"Justin, get your big paws off me," Holly yelled, glaring down at him.

"Oh, no, ma'am," he said, smiling. "I was raised to help ladies in distress, and you were about to fall off that ladder. Just go right ahead with your dusting, and I'll hold you nice and steady. Pretend I'm not here."

What could she do? The heat from his hands around her waist was incredible. Now he was moving his hands to caress her stomach, her hips. She couldn't give him the satisfaction of knowing he was driving her mad.

Justin stifled a groan as Holly began wiggling more than necessary. Two could play this game, and now heated desire rocketed through him. He was dying, and she knew it, the minx.

"Done," she said. But before she could step down, Justin hauled her into his arms and drew her close, her feet still dangling.

"Put me down!" she insisted. But as soon as her feet touched the floor, his lips claimed hers in a soul-shattering kiss. . . .

WHAT ARE *LOVESWEPT* ROMANCES?

They are stories of true romance and touching emotion. We believe those two very important ingredients are constants in our highly sensual and very believable stories in the *LOVESWEPT* line. Our goal is to give you, the reader, stories of consistently high quality that may sometimes make you laugh, sometimes make you cry, but are always fresh and creative and contain many delightful surprises within their pages.

Most romance fans read an enormous number of books. Those they truly love, they keep. Others may be traded with friends and soon forgotten. We hope that each *LOVESWEPT* romance will be a treasure—a "keeper." We will always try to publish

LOVE STORIES YOU'LL NEVER FORGET
BY AUTHORS YOU'LL ALWAYS REMEMBER

The Editors

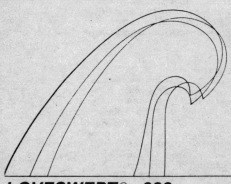

LOVESWEPT® • 332

Joan Elliott Pickart
Holly's Hope

 BANTAM BOOKS
NEW YORK • TORONTO • LONDON • SYDNEY • AUCKLAND

HOLLY'S HOPE

A Bantam Book / June 1989

LOVESWEPT® and the wave device are registered
trademarks of Bantam Books, a division of
Bantam Doubleday Dell Publishing Group, Inc.
Registered in U.S. Patent
and Trademark Office and elsewhere.

If you would be interested in receiving protective vinyl
covers for your Loveswept books, please write to this address
for information:

Loveswept
Bantam Books
P.O. Box 985
Hicksville, NY 11802

ISBN 0-553-22010-1

Published simultaneously in the United States and Canada

Bantam Books are published by Bantam Books, a division
of Bantam Doubleday Dell Publishing Group, Inc. Its trademark, consisting of the words "Bantam Books" and the
portrayal of a rooster, is Registered in U.S. Patent and
Trademark Office and in other countries. Marca Registrada.
Bantam Books, 666 Fifth Avenue, New York, New York 10103.

PRINTED IN THE UNITED STATES OF AMERICA

O   0 9 8 7 6 5 4 3 2 1

For Ed . . . just because

One

She was dead.

Holly Chambers sighed, closed her eyes, and laced her fingers together on her stomach. The carpet of sweet-smelling grass on which she lay was quite comfortable, she admitted, and the warm spring sun pouring over her felt heavenly.

But, darn it, she didn't want to be dead!

It wasn't fair, she decided, and she was going to speak to Charlie Potts about this. She'd been dead last year, too, and it seemed to her that being dead should be passed around a bit.

Holly wiggled a little in the grass as though she were in her own bed at home and tuned out the loud noises around her.

Being dead wasn't so bad, she supposed. She could totally ignore the hubbub of activity, the yelling and confusion, and concentrate instead on the buzzing of a bee somewhere in the distance.

And she was very, very comfy lying in the plush grass with her own waterfall of sunshine.

Very comfy . . . and rather deliciously hazy. That lovely, floaty feeling she always got just . . . before she . . . fell . . . asleep.

Justin Hope drove slowly down the street, frowning as he glanced around. He'd rented a car at the airport sixty miles away and driven above the speed limit to his destination. The weather-beaten sign at the edge of town had said, "Welcome to Maple Tree, Wisconsin," so he knew he was in the right place. It was an attractive little town with huge shade trees lining the streets, and looked like a place that people cared about and took pride in.

But where were the people?

He hadn't seen a living soul except for a fat dog who'd been plodding along the sidewalk. There were cars parked in front of a row of small stores, but no people!

Strange, Justin thought, like a scene out of *The Twilight Zone*. It was the middle of the afternoon on a warm spring day and people should be out and about. So where was everyone?

He turned a corner and went another block, driving at a crawl. Nothing. No one. Even the fat dog had disappeared.

What in the hell was going on here, he wondered. The report he'd gotten on Maple Tree, Wisconsin, had stated that it was a small lakeside town that made its revenue from the tourists who came to fish in both summer and winter. It was a popular vacation spot for those wishing to escape from the frantic pace of the big cities. It had a population of between three and four thousand, including those living on farms in the outlying countryside.

Oh, really? Justin thought. Well, they'd all been whisked away by an alien spaceship, or gone out to lunch with E.T., or something, because there were no people in Maple Tree, Wisconsin!

Wonderful, he fumed. This really capped it. He was blurry with fatigue, nearly numb with worry and icy fear. And over the past six weeks anger had begun to build within him as well, crashing against the other depleting emotions Melinda had roused in him.

He took a left at the next corner and continued driving slowly. Suddenly his eyes widened and he slammed on the brakes, throwing himself forward against the steering wheel.

"My God," he whispered in horror.

His gaze swept over a large grassy field adjacent to what appeared to be a school. People were running in all directions, and ambulances, police cars, and fire trucks were lined up in a row.

And on the ground was a multitude of bodies!

A roaring noise filled Justin's ears as he forced himself into action. He parked his car against the curb and vaulted from it, starting to run the moment his feet hit the street.

A catastrophe had hit Maple Tree, he thought, and Melinda might be in this town! What had happened here? A fire? Gas leak? Poisoned water? The possibilities were endless and frightening.

He entered the field through an opening in the chain-link fence, his feet thudding in a steady rhythm. People were shouting orders and dashing in all directions, and the sound of cries and moans hung heavily in the air. An ambulance wailed and sped away from the scene with lights flashing.

As he ran, Justin took in the nightmare, then he stopped abruptly, nearly toppling over. He'd almost run right into a body. His heart pounding wildly, he dropped to his knees beside the motionless young woman.

Calm down, he told himself. He'd only be in the way if he went searching for Melinda now. As difficult as it was, he'd have to wait. In the meantime, maybe he could help somehow even though he had no idea what was wrong with these people.

He focused on the woman lying before him. He guessed she was in her mid-twenties, and she had short, curly blond hair. Dressed in jeans and a red cotton blouse, she was slender and of average height. Her features were delicate. She was really quite beautiful in a fresh, wholesome way.

And dead?

Justin rested his hands on his thighs and leaned over, peering closely at the woman. She had a serene expression on her face, and her long lashes were fanned on her lightly tanned cheeks. His gaze slid lower, and he was momentarily mesmerized by the slow and steady rise and fall of her breasts.

She was breathing, he realized. She was alive. Her pretty hands were folded on her stomach as though someone were about to close the coffin, but this beautiful young woman was alive.

"I need a stretcher over here," someone yelled. "Stat."

"Help me. Help me," a woman moaned in the distance.

"I'm losing him," another man shouted. "Get oxygen."

Justin pulled his mind from the chaos around him and concentrated on the woman. Her breathing was still even, and he couldn't discern any visible injury. She appeared to be enjoying a nap in the sunshine, which was absurd, of course, because there was something terribly wrong with her. But what?

Dammit, he thought, why hadn't he taken that first aid class at the health club where he worked out when he had time? He'd decided he was too busy then. And now here he was, staring at a lovely young woman who needed his help, and he didn't know what to do.

He tentatively lifted one hand and placed it on the woman's cheek. Her skin was warm. And soft. Very soft. She had a natural peaches-and-cream complexion. Her lips were slightly parted, as if she were waiting to be kissed. By him.

He stroked the woman's cheek with his thumb. Her skin was like velvet, he mused. Or rose petals. Or . . .

Heat rocketed through his body, twisting low and heavy within him, and he jerked his hand away in self-disgust.

Lord, he thought, she could draw her last breath at any moment, and he was reacting to her on a sexual level. Shock. Yes, he was in shock. Justin Hope didn't pant after women like an adolescent.

"Do something constructive," he ordered himself, then leaned over until his face was inches from the woman's. "Hello? Can you hear me?"

Holly foggily decided to ignore the voice disturbing her sleep. She was in the middle of a delicious dream where she was standing in front of a seven-foot hot fudge sundae complete with mounds of whipped cream and an enormous cherry. In the distance she could see a waitress walking toward her, carrying a spoon bigger than a baseball bat. Any minute now Holly would have that spoon and her first bite of the tempting ice cream.

"Hello?"

Oh, go away, Holly thought. The owner of that deep, rich voice was rude. That male voice. That sexy voice. Who on earth owned that incredible voice she'd never heard before? To find out, she'd have to wake up and watch the hot fudge sundae disappear into oblivion. And she hadn't even had a bite of it yet. Forget it. She was staying with the ice cream.

"Please. Try to open your eyes."

Then again, Holly pondered hazily, a person could always find a hot fudge sundae. Not one that was seven feet tall, of course, but she'd probably be sick as a dog if she ate it, anyway. It was not, however, every day of the week that a voice like the one she was hearing pleaded with her to wake up. No contest. The voice was the winner.

She slowly opened her eyes, blinked, then gasped as she stared at the face so close to hers.

She had never in her life seen such a handsome man. He had high cheekbones and a straight nose.

His skin was deeply tanned, his hair thick and dark as night, and his eyes were a vivid blue surrounded by spiky dark lashes. His lips were beautiful, kissable and beautiful, and his chin was square and strong. This man was more scrumptious than a hot fudge sundae as big as a silo.

"Thank goodness, you're awake," he said. "Can you tell me what's wrong with you?"

She couldn't breathe, Holly thought. That was what was wrong with her. The air had seemed to swish from her lungs the moment she'd gazed into those incredible blue eyes. A strange sensation of heat started tingling deep within her.

"Try to speak," the man said. "What happened to you?"

"I'm dead," she said, totally amazed that any sound had come out of her mouth.

He grabbed one of her hands and cradled it between his. "No, no, you're not dead. Don't even think such a thing."

Such big, strong hands he had, she thought, gazing at those hands. Warm, marvelous hands. His fingers were long and tanned, his nails perfectly trimmed. He was wearing a blue shirt that did terrific things for his eyes, and a paisley print tie.

Her gaze skittered lower. Dark slacks pulled across his muscular thighs as he knelt beside her. He was obviously tall, and had wide shoulders. And that voice. Oh, good heavens, that voice.

"I—" she started, then stopped and cleared her throat. "I really am dead. I had my dead card, but I dropped it somewhere because I was in such a snit. I just didn't think it was fair that I had to be dead two years in a row."

"Did you get hit on the head?" he asked, tightening his hold on her hand. "You're not making any sense. I wonder if that's a symptom of a concussion." He looked across the field for a moment, then met her gaze again. "I'll have to go see if I can get someone to come over here and help you. Will you be all right if I leave you alone for a minute?"

"No, they won't come over here. Everyone saw Charlie Potts give me my dead card. He's going to be mad as a hornet that I dropped it, but that's just too darn bad. He told me last year, when we helped him meet his disaster drill quota, that I could be wounded this time and get to ride in an ambulance. But did he keep his word? No, not Charlie Potts. Brother, am I going to give him a piece of my mind."

The man stiffened. "Disaster drill? Drill?" He narrowed his eyes, and a frown knitted his dark brows. "Are you telling me that all of this madness is pretend, a charade? There hasn't been a god-awful catastrophe here?"

She smiled brightly. "We're a plane crash. Last year we were a huge pileup of smashed cars, but Charlie got jazzy this time." She frowned. "I swear, I'm going to refuse to volunteer next year unless Charlie solemnly promises to let me be wounded. I'm sick to death of being dead." She paused and smiled again. "I'm Holly Chambers. Are you just passing through Maple Tree, or did you come to fish?"

Justin dropped Holly's hand, which he realized

he was still holding, and lunged to his feet. "Dammit, I can't believe this. A drill. None of you people are hurt, it's all a game?"

Holly struggled to stand up. She planted her hands on her hips, absently registering the fact that the man was over six feet tall, and glared at him.

"This is no game, Mr. . . . whoever you are."

"Hope. Justin Hope," he said, glaring right back. "Did it ever occur to you that someone might think that this"—he swept one arm through the air—"was real? You took ten years off my life, lady."

"Oh, is that so? Well, there's a sign hanging on the front of the school, Mr. Justin Hope, that says 'Emergency Services Disaster Drill.' "

"Do you think I should have stopped to see if there was a sign saying this was a game?" Justin asked, his voice rising. "I thought you were hurt."

"I was dead, you dolt!"

He stared up at the sky for a long moment as he struggled to rein in his temper. Where had that angry outburst come from? He was a man of control, his emotions under his command at all times. Somewhere in the midst of this ridiculous situation there might be a humorous side, but at the moment he couldn't see it. He was mad as hell, pure and simple.

There he stood, business tycoon Justin Hope, with a beautiful pint-sized woman insisting that she was dead. Not hurt, not needing his help, but deader than a doornail because some joker named Charlie hadn't kept his promise to let her ride in an ambulance.

The people in this town were insane! And Melinda was somewhere among these nut cases, he realized. Well, in all fairness, Holly Chambers was a very pretty nut case, with big brown eyes, like a fawn's. And he liked her name. It conjured up images of a cozy fire as snow fell outside, snifters of brandy, and making love in the glow of Christmas tree lights. Lord above, listen to him. He was so jarred he was having syrupy, romantic thoughts. This was absurd. Enough was enough.

"Miss Chambers," he said, looking at her again, "I—"

"Mrs. Chambers," she said stiffly.

A wave of what was recognizably disappointment swept through Justin. He dismissed it instantly, telling himself it was just another off-the-wall reaction to what he'd been through. He didn't care whether or not Holly Chambers was married.

But why wasn't she wearing any rings, he wondered. It didn't fit the image of the small-town wife and mother. Maybe Holly Chambers had a policy to never wear her wedding ring when she was going to be in a plane crash. Oh, forget it.

"I suppose your husband is out there running around with the rest of those people," Justin said. "Did he get to ride in an ambulance? Poor guy. You'll probably give him hell if he got to enjoy that thrill-a-minute adventure and you didn't."

Holly lifted her chin. "I'm a widow, Mr. Hope."

He felt as though he'd been punched in the stomach. "I'm sorry," he said quietly. "I was way out of line with what I just said. I apologize."

"You had no way of knowing," she said, "and, besides, I've been a widow for a long time. You didn't upset me." She paused. "I owe you an apology, too, Mr. Hope. I'm beginning to see what a shock it must have been to come upon a scene like this. I should be thanking you for trying to help me, not yelling at you that you could have read a sign on a door half a block away." She laughed. "You must have thought I was totally deranged when I kept insisting I was dead."

She had a lovely laugh, Justin thought, and her smile was as sparkling as the spring sunshine. Good Lord, where was all this poetic nonsense coming from?

Before he could think of a reply to her statement, a voice boomed through the air.

"Attention! Attention! Attention!"

Holly rolled her eyes. "That's Charlie Potts. He gets a big charge out of yelling through the police bullhorn. I think it's the high point of his whole year."

"The drill is over," Charlie bellowed. "All victims were attended to in seventy-one minutes. That's two minutes better than last year. Congratulations, and thank you one and all. Over and out."

"Over and out?" Justin muttered under his breath.

"I'd like a word with you, Charlie Potts," Holly called, planting her hands on her hips again.

Uh-oh, Justin thought. Potts better head for the hills.

A tall, thin man in his late twenties loped across the field to Holly and Justin. He wore thick glasses, had thinning brown hair, and a toothy grin.

"It was great, Holly," Charlie said, breathing heavily from his run. "I met the state requirement of four drills, and Maple Tree had a better score time than the hospital in Madison. This is going to look terrific in my personnel file."

Holly smiled. "That's wonderful, Charlie. I know how hard you've worked to—" She frowned. "Oh, I forgot. Don't speak to me. One cannot carry on a conversation with a dead person. And I am dead. Again. Two years in a row. You said I could be wounded. Why, pray tell, did you break your promise to me?"

Charlie glanced at Justin.

"Oh, just ignore me," Justin said, raising a hand. "Pretend I'm not here."

"Charlie, this is Justin Hope," Holly said. "He thought the drill was real. I think you need to have a bigger sign. We could get some poster board and colored markers and—darn it, stay on the subject. Why was I dead? Oh, and I lost my dead card. It's gone, poof, disappeared."

"You lost your dead card?" Charlie said. "How could you do such a thing? That's state property, Holly Chambers."

"Tough tomatoes, Charlie Potts. You owe me an explanation."

Why was he still standing there, Justin asked himself. He should be tracking down Melinda, not waiting around to see the outcome of a ridiculous squabble between this beautiful terror and a tall, skinny version of Bucky Beaver. Arguments in Justin Hope's world concerned millions of dollars, not insanity like who did or didn't get a dead card. He was leaving. Now.

"Well?" Holly said. "Speak, Potts."

Dammit, Justin thought, he wasn't leaving now,

and he knew it. He'd go crazy if he didn't see how this turned out. Tough tomatoes? Holly Chambers was really something.

"Don't be mad at me, Holly," Charlie said. His voice dropped to a whisper. "Clara Mary went to the movies with me Saturday night. I've been asking and asking her, and she finally said yes. Then Sunday she had me to supper. Clara Mary, Holly, can you believe that? When she said she wanted to be wounded instead of dead in the plane crash I . . . well, I . . . I've loved Clara Mary ever since second grade. She said she'd go to the movies with me again Saturday night. That's a good sign, don't you think? I mean, considering the fact that the same movie will be showing for a month."

Justin covered his burst of laughter by coughing behind his hand. "Excuse me," he said. "I had something in my throat. Go right on with what you were saying, Charlie."

Both Holly and Charlie looked at him, and he smiled pleasantly.

"Clara Mary?" Holly said, redirecting her attention to Charlie.

"She's my heart's desire," Charlie said with a sigh, laying one hand on his chest.

"Ever since second grade," Justin interjected. Holly glared at him, and he shrugged. "Sorry."

"Clara Mary," Holly repeated. "My goodness, I had no idea you cared for her, Charlie. That is so sweet, so romantic. All these years you've worshiped her from afar, and she's finally seen you for the wonderful, dynamic man that you are."

"I am?" Charlie said.

"He is?" Justin said.

"A woman doesn't see *Invasion of the Giant Fruit Flies* twice unless she's smitten with her escort," Holly said.

"Good point," Justin said, nodding.

"Then you understand why I let *her* be wounded instead of you?" Charlie asked.

"Oh, my, yes," Holly said. "Don't give it another thought. I adore romance, and your story about you and Clara Mary is so romantic that it's enough to make me weep. You will keep me posted, won't you?"

"Sure thing, Holly."

"I'm sorry I lost my dead card, Charlie. It's out there on the field somewhere, unless it got trampled to pieces."

"I'll look for it. Thanks, Holly. I gotta go." Charlie turned and ran back to his "command post."

"Clara Mary and Charlie Potts," Holly said with a wistful sigh. "Oh, that is just so romantic. I hope it works out for them. They've both been alone for too long."

"You're really into romance, aren't you?" Justin said.

She looked up at him. "Oh, yes. I hear a story like Charlie just told and I feel warm inside. Think about it. Two lonely people could very well be on their way to happiness together. Don't you agree that it's wonderful?"

"I suppose, providing that's what they want. Not everyone is cut out for commitment, marriage, that sort of thing."

"It sounds like you're talking about yourself."

He nodded. "I run a business that takes most of my energy and time, and I enjoy that. I'm not interested in getting seriously involved with a woman." He paused. "I assume that since you get so caught up in romance that there's someone special in your life?"

Why had he asked her that, he wondered. It made no difference whatsoever to him who Holly Chambers might be involved with.

"No," she answered quickly. She shifted her gaze to somewhere over his left shoulder. "Well, I must be going. It was nice meeting you, Justin. I'm sorry your introduction to Maple Tree was so unsettling. It's really a very lovely, quiet little town. Good-bye." She spun around and started away.

"Wait a minute."

She turned to look at him. "Yes?"

"Maybe you can help me. I'm looking for someone named Melinda."

A woman, Holly thought. He had come to Maple Tree in search of a woman. Well, it was none of her business. A man like Justin Hope no doubt had a waiting list of women hoping to spend time with him. In his bed? Probably.

She couldn't stop her gaze from roaming over his marvelous body. What would it be like to make love with him, she wondered. He had an aura of command and authority about him, and she imagined he would be a demanding lover. But would he make certain of her pleasure before he— Her? Who? Oh, for heaven's sake, what a silly conversation to be having with herself.

"Holly?"

"What? Oh, no, I don't know anyone named Melinda, but a lot of tourists come and go through Maple Tree."

"She was seen getting off a bus here two weeks ago, but then she disappeared. I was in London when I heard, and returned to the States as quickly as I could." He frowned and dragged a hand through his hair. "Maybe she's long gone, I don't know. I just had to come here myself and search for her. I have to find her. I have to."

There was an edge of panic to his voice, and she saw a flicker of pain in his eyes. In the next instant, though, he stiffened and seemed to draw a curtain over his features, no longer giving any clues to his emotions.

But she'd seen it, she thought, the vulnerability, the helplessness. She guessed Justin Hope was used to being in control of all and everything, yet there was a chink in his armor.

He was a complicated man, she mused. He'd set aside his mission of finding Melinda to rush to Holly's aid when he thought she was hurt. He'd allowed his sense of humor to surface briefly when she'd demanded an explanation from Charlie Potts for declaring her dead. And now she'd seen his anxiety as he spoke about the woman he had to find. There were, indeed, many layers to Justin, depths that she somehow knew few people were given a glimpse of. Very, very complicated.

"Justin," she said, "perhaps if you described Melinda to me, I might remember having seen her. She's obviously very important to you, and I'd like to help if I can."

"Important?" he repeated with a bark of laughter. He felt as though his mind had just clicked off, granting him a short reprieve from his fear and anger. It was all rushing back on him now, slamming against his mind with renewed force. "She's all I have. I love her, although it's quite apparent she doesn't believe that."

Holly frowned. "But you said you didn't have time for a romantic involvement." She shook her head. "Never mind. I don't mean to pry. You love Melinda, and if she's in Maple Tree, we'll find her. You two can talk, work things out—"

"Hold it," Justin interrupted, raising one hand. His jaw was set in a hard line, and his eyes were narrowed. "You think this is another oh-so-wonderful love story, don't you?"

"Why are you suddenly angry at *me*?" she asked. "All I'm trying to do is help you find Melinda. You said that you love her, you flew all the way from London to search for her here. You're not making any sense. Why should you care if I find that very romantic? What I think isn't important. Finding Melinda is what matters to you. You're a man in love who—"

His hands shot out and he gripped her upper arms. "You're painting a picture of me that's all wrong, Holly Chambers," he said through clenched teeth. "Don't stuff me into a syrupy-sweet romantic scenario like Clara Mary and Bucky Beaver. I would not *ever* chase halfway around the world to find a woman!"

Holly stared up at him. "But you said—"

"I know what I said, and you've jumped to conclusions, seeing this whole thing through rose-colored glasses. Well, I'm not part of your little romantic world. What do you do when you come face-to-face with a man who walks, talks, and breathes in the *real* world?"

"Let go of me, Justin Hope. Go find your beloved Melinda and leave me alone."

"No. I want an answer to my question. How do you deal with reality? How do you deal with this?"

Her startled gasp was smothered by his mouth coming down hard on hers. As he pulled her close to him, she flattened her hands on his chest and pushed away with all her might. Her efforts produced nothing except the message to her brain that beneath her palms was hard muscle and a great deal of strength.

Justin's kiss gentled almost instantly. His lips were soft against hers, and his tongue had somehow slipped into her mouth and was exploring every dark crevice.

Her eyes drifted closed as her hands floated up to encircle his neck. She leaned farther into him, responding to his kiss, drinking in his taste, inhaling his aroma. Heat pulsed low within her, then swept throughout her, burning away the warnings from her conscience that she shouldn't be doing this.

Never, she thought hazily, had she been kissed like this. Never had she felt such an instant flame of desire. Her breasts ached with a strange heaviness, a wish to be soothed by Justin's hands. A tide of sensations was carrying her away to a place she'd never been. A frightening yet exciting place. A place she shouldn't be traveling to, but, oh, how she wanted to go. With Justin.

Dear Lord, Justin thought, what in the hell was he doing? He hadn't intended to kiss Holly Chambers. But he *was* kissing her, and he didn't want to stop. She tasted so good, felt so good, and the blood was thundering in his veins. She was responding to him totally, and he wanted more. He wanted her naked beneath him, giving and receiving, as he joined his body with hers. Never before had he felt such a driving, burning need to make love with a woman. He wanted Holly. Right now.

Hope, his mind screamed, *get control!* He didn't behave this way. He was punchy with fatigue from jet lag, from the long weeks spent worrying about Melinda, and from the anger that was tightening within him like a fist.

He had reached the end of his rope and wasn't acting like himself. In his weary state he'd blown everything out of proportion and had become momentarily obsessed with the need to be certain Holly saw him as a man, a real man, not some romantic figure like Charlie Potts.

And so he'd kissed her. Now he wanted her.

No more, he told himself. He had to stop kissing Holly before he slipped over the edge. His mind and body were always under his command. He'd been a victim of his own emotions and fatigue, but he was back in control now. He was Justin Hope, dammit, and he didn't do things like this.

He tore his mouth from Holly's and stepped back. He drew a deep, steadying breath, willed his heart to quiet its wild beating, and forced a bland expression onto his face. Then he groaned inwardly as he stared at Holly, at her kiss-swollen lips and the smoky hue of desire in her brown eyes.

Their gazes held for a long moment as currents

of sexuality crackled between them, wound around them, and urged them to move back into each other's embrace.

Justin took another step away and cleared his throat, breaking the sensual spell.

Holly filled her lungs with the fresh spring air and glanced around to assure herself she was still standing in the familiar grassy field. Her mind was a buzzing jumble of confusion while her body still hummed with desire. She could feel passion's flush on her cheeks.

Oh, how she wished she could rant and rave, pitch a fit, accuse Justin of taking advantage of her. But she knew she couldn't do that because she'd participated in that kiss, had returned Justin's ardor in total abandon. Why? She didn't know. Nor did she know why Justin's kiss had stirred something new and amazingly powerful within her. She was such a befuddled mess, she wasn't even sure she felt any guilt over her wanton behavior.

"Well," she started, then threw up her hands in defeat. "Never mind. I have absolutely no idea what to say to you, Justin. I could go on and on, I suppose, about how I don't kiss men I just met, that I don't, in fact, kiss anyone the way I did you. But you'd have no reason to believe me because I obviously just did what I would declare that I never do. Did that make sense? Probably not. Nothing is making sense to me right now."

"That makes us even, Holly," Justin said quietly, looking directly into her eyes. "I don't normally behave like I did, either. I could plead jet lag, emotional fatigue from worrying about Melinda, but I won't. I think it would be best if we both forgot what just happened." Could he do that? Could he forget that kiss, Holly's taste, the softness of her slender body? Could he dismiss the ache still throbbing deep within him? "Okay?"

Forget that kiss, the desire, the heat? Holly asked herself. No, she didn't think she could do that. "Okay," she said softly. "Fine." She managed a small smile. "Melinda. Yes, it's time to get back to the business at hand. You want very much to find Melinda because"—her smile faded—"because you love her."

He nodded. "Yes, I love her very much. But it's not what you think, Holly. You automatically assumed this was a wonderfully romantic tale of a man flying halfway around the world to find his woman, his lover. It isn't like that, not even close."

"Then why are you here? I don't understand, Justin."

"Holly, Melinda is my sixteen-year-old sister. She ran away almost six weeks ago, and I've been out of my mind with worry. I have to find her, don't you see? I have to find my baby sister!"

Two

Dozens of thoughts tumbled rapidly through Holly's mind, intertwining with the confusion already churning there. Her bafflement over kissing Justin was pushed aside to make room for her reactions to his impassioned statement about Melinda.

Her heart sang with joy for a fleeting moment as she realized he was not in Maple Tree in search of the love of his life. But before she could examine that euphoric reaction, a rush of guilt dropped over her like a dark cloud.

Melinda was a teenager, an unhappy young girl who had run away. And Justin was nearly consumed with worry, fear, and pain. She wanted to hold him in her arms, comfort him, assure him that they would find his sister and end his nightmare.

Her rambling thoughts were cut short by his voice.

"I've spent enough time standing in this field," he said.

He was doing it again, Holly realized. The curtain was in place over his features once more, giving no hint to his inner turmoil. He'd straightened his stance, squared his shoulders, and erected a barrier around himself.

He was making it clear with body language and a cool glint in his eyes that she was not to intrude into his space, his private hell. He was, she guessed, angry at himself that he had momentarily dropped his guard and given her a glimpse of his vulnerability. Oh, yes, Justin Hope was a complicated man, but she was slowly beginning to understand at least a few of the many facets of him.

One thing she knew with crystal clarity; she wanted to learn all the complexities that made up this man.

"Justin," she said, "what does Melinda look like? Do you have a picture of her? Maybe I've seen her."

Justin gazed at her for a long moment, seeming at war within himself. He finally nodded and reached in his back pocket for his wallet. He took out a photograph and handed it to Holly.

She gasped and her eyes widened. "Missy Hopkins."

"What?"

"Justin, this girl is Missy Hopkins. She came to my place, Holly's Bed and Breakfast, two weeks ago. She said she was eighteen and was looking for work."

"Did you hire her?" he asked, aware that he was hardly breathing. "Is she still there?"

"Yes."

Justin closed his eyes for a moment to regain control of his emotions. "Thank God," he whispered. "I've found her." He looked at Holly again. "My car is parked at the end of the block. Come on, let's go. Show me where Melinda is." He turned and started away.

Holly hurried after him, placing a hand on his forearm to halt his step. "Justin, wait."

He stopped and looked down at her. "Wait for what? I finally know where Melinda is after all these weeks. I'm going to go get her."

"And do what?" Holly asked, dropping her hand. "Throw her over your shoulder and carry her kicking and screaming back to . . . wherever it is you live?"

"New York," he said, his jaw tight, "in a huge apartment overlooking Central Park. Our parents were killed two years ago and I was named her legal guardian. She's enrolled in a top-quality private school, and has an allowance large enough to satisfy her every whim. A housekeeper lives in the apartment, so Melinda isn't alone when I travel. When I'm home I take her to dinner at the finest restaurants, get tickets to Broadway shows, ballets, whatever she wants."

"*When* you're home? How often is that, Justin? You said that you flew here from London. How long had you been there? If you counted up the days in this year, how many of them would you have spent with Melinda?"

"Dammit, I have an investment company to run.

A multimillion-dollar corporation that requires my attention and presence all over the world. That company, by the way, is what provides Melinda with the finest money can buy. So, okay, maybe I'm not home much, but when I am I devote every minute to her. We share quality time, which all the books I've read on parenting say is very important. I love Melinda, I'm with her when I can be, I give her every material thing she even hints at. Lord, what more can I do? What does she want from me? I can't be cloned, can't be in two places at once. She's old enough to realize that. She left a note saying she was lonely and unhappy, so she was leaving. Just like that." He snapped his fingers. "Gone. Can you believe that?"

"Yes."

"Oh, thanks a helluva lot," Justin said with a snort of disgust. "I'm the bad guy here, right? Shame on me for working eighteen-hour days, knocking myself out to make a success of Hope Enterprises, for providing a secure present and future for myself and my sister. Oh, yeah, that's really rotten of me. Just put the rope around my neck, declare me guilty, and be done with it. Never mind that the judge and jury is a sixteen-year-old kid who's acting like a spoiled brat. I'm not defending myself to you, Holly Chambers, not for another minute. I'm going to go get my sister and take her home." He strode away.

"You're making a terrible mistake, Justin," Holly called after him.

He stopped dead in his tracks, his back to her, and she could see the muscles in his body tense. She was pushing him to the limit of his patience, and the edge of his temper, and she knew it. Justin was tired, Holly thought, both physically and mentally, and wanted nothing more than to find his sister at long last, take her home, then get on with his life. But he was going about it all wrong!

"Justin, please, listen to me for just one minute. Please?"

He turned slowly to face her, and she inwardly cringed when she saw the anger radiating from his eyes.

She swallowed heavily before attempting to speak. "You said that Melinda disappeared after she got to Maple Tree. She did disappear in a sense, inside Holly's Bed and Breakfast. She's hardly been out of the door since she arrived. I give her a room and meals in exchange for doing odd jobs for me. I've never had any reason to ask her to prove if she is Missy Hopkins."

"What's the point you're trying to make?" Justin asked stiffly.

"I realize now that she didn't go out because she didn't want to be found. I'm sorry if it hurts you to hear that, but she's obviously been hiding. Oh, Justin, she's so sad. I've heard her crying in her room at night, and she rarely smiles. I've tried to talk to her, get her to open up and share with me. She's come close, but then she shuts an invisible door, hides her emotions just—just like you do. Maybe she *is* spoiled by all the possessions she has, I don't know. What I do know is that she's a very unhappy girl. I look at her and my heart just aches."

"That figures," Justin said, shaking his head.

"She's a pathetic heroine in one of your other-world fantasies. You get weepy over Clara Mary seeing some fruit-fly movie twice. Poor little Melinda must put your imagination in overdrive. I can just picture the tragic scenarios you've concocted about her and what she's crying about."

"Damn you, Justin Hope," Holly yelled. "You are the most stubborn, narrow-minded man I've ever met. You just charge in full-steam-ahead, the consequences be hanged. Well, I'm telling you this, mister. You may be the all and everything in the corporate world, but what you know about sixteen-year-old girls isn't worth diddly. Melinda's tears are real. Her unhappiness is real. If you storm the gates and drag her out, you will have accomplished nothing."

"I'll have her back home where she belongs," he said, matching her volume.

"For how long? Do you think she ran away to gain your attention, get you to jump as she pulled the strings? Wrong. She didn't want to be found, remember? She's been hiding at my place like a fugitive who's afraid she'll be discovered. Slow down, Justin, and think."

"Why don't *you* slow down and think," he shot back, "about whether or not this is any of your damn business."

Justin's brutal words were like a dash of cold water being flung over Holly. Tears burned at the back of her eyes and misery chilled her within.

"Yes, of course," she said, her voice trembling, "you're absolutely right. This is between you and Melinda. You're family, the two of you. I shouldn't be intruding where I don't belong. I—I'm sorry. If you . . . um, go back to the main street of town, and turn left at the second light, you'll be on Christmas Lane. My place is halfway down the block on the right. That's where you'll find Melinda." She turned and started away. "Good-bye, Justin. Good luck."

Dammit, Justin thought, why had he been so cruel to Holly? Her big brown eyes had looked so sad, almost brimming with tears, and she'd had a stricken expression on her face as though he'd struck her. Where in the hell was his control? One emotion after another had surfaced in the past half hour, the last being anger, which had hurt Holly. She'd only been trying to help, and he'd hurled her generosity and caring nature back at her like bruising stones.

He watched as she walked across the field. He felt a strange sense of loss and emptiness along with a chilling loneliness. It was as though by her leaving, Holly had taken with her the warmth and freshness of the spring day.

He'd never met anyone like Holly Chambers before, he realized. She seemed to have an open door to her heart, and was ready to receive the joy or sorrow of everyone who touched her life. She'd been sincerely happy for Charlie Potts and his conquest of Clara Mary. And she cared, really cared, that Melinda cried alone in her room at night.

She gave and gave, but did she ever take? Did she ever take the love of a man?

When he'd asked her if there was someone special in her life, she had been quick to say no, then change the subject. She'd appeared uncomfortable with the question, had even averted her eyes from his. Why? Was she still mourning her dead husband? He didn't think so. The mention of him hadn't upset her, and she'd said she'd been a widow for a long time.

His hands shoved into the front pockets of his slacks, Justin walked slowly across the field toward his car. It was difficult to remember that he had just met Holly. He felt changed somehow, as though his outward shield had been stripped away, revealing to Holly the inner depths of his being. Would he be kidding himself if he chalked up his reaction to Holly to fatigue? He didn't know.

And that kiss, he thought as he got into his car, had been real, honest. The mere remembrance of it caused him to ache anew with the need to make love with Holly until they were both sated and too exhausted to move.

Dammit, Justin thought, lightly hitting the steering wheel. What was it about that pint-sized woman with the big brown eyes and silky blond curls? Why couldn't he just dismiss her from his mind? Why did he feel like the villain of the year for causing the hurt he'd seen on her face? Why in the hell did she matter so much to him?

"Enough, Hope," he said, turning the key in the ignition. He was going to go get his sister and forget about Holly Chambers. He was going to take Melinda home, where she belonged, and forget about Holly Chambers. When he left this town, he'd erase it from his memory, and Holly Chambers along with it.

Wouldn't he?

• • •

As Holly walked along Christmas Lane, she glanced around at the big old houses and the huge trees that stood like silent sentries. She saw the green lawns and the first flowers pushing above the ground, eager to reach the spring sunshine that welcomed them. She heard the birds singing and children's laughter.

Familiar things, all of them, known to her for many years. Yet she felt as though she had stepped out of herself and was viewing her surroundings for the first time. The sights, sounds and smells were richer, more vivid. Everything seemed magnified, her senses razor-sharp.

She shivered, not liking this eerie sensation. And not liking the fact that the image of Justin Hope flitted back and forth in her mind.

As she had walked away from him, she'd been determined to dismiss as unimportant the chilling hurt she had felt when he'd told her to mind her own business. She had vowed to forget the kiss they had shared. She'd promised herself that she'd erase from her mind her fleeting interlude with Justin, as though it had never happened.

Holly sighed. So much for noble intentions, she thought dismally. Justin had apparently taken up permanent residency in her mind.

And in her heart?

Oh, that was absurd, she told herself. She had met the man less than an hour earlier. But why did it seem as though she'd known him for a lifetime? Why did she feel detached from herself, and different from the person who had set out earlier to become a victim of the staged plane crash? Why did she feel hollow and lonely because

Justin had sent her away, feel that she had had something special, rare, and beautiful for a fleeting moment, only to have it torn from her grasp and crushed into dust?

"Really absurd," she muttered, deciding to stomp along the sidewalk instead of just strolling. She was beginning to sound like the romantic fruitcake Justin had wrongly accused her of being. Of course she enjoyed watching romance happen between people she knew and cared about. There was nothing weird about that. But she did not ever fantasize about a romantic interlude that starred her and an imaginary, faceless man.

"No, no, no," she said, shaking her head. She had loved once, long ago, given all of herself to a man. Never again. She dated on occasion, but gently told any man who hinted at wanting more that she just wasn't interested.

And, she vowed, the image of Justin in her mind, the memories of him, his kiss, his magnificent body, and incredibly handsome face, had better get the message, too, and leave her alone!

"Yoo-hoo, Holly," a voice called. "How was the plane crash?"

Holly stopped and dragged her mind from its tangled maze of jumbled thoughts. She looked over to see an elderly woman standing in her front yard wearing a bright pink cotton dress, a perky sunbonnet, and gardening gloves.

"Hello, Mrs. Hill," Holly called. "The plane crash was a huge success. Charlie Potts is in seventh heaven."

"Wonderful. Oh, do tell your father hello for me. My tulips are coming up, Holly. Don't you adore spring, when everything wakes up from the long sleep of winter?"

"Yes, spring is lovely. See you later, Mrs. Hill," Holly said, and started off again.

The long sleep of winter, she repeated silently. Spring was when everything woke up. Justin's kiss had awakened within her a desire she'd thought long dead. Had it only been slumbering in the winter chill within her, waiting for a special touch, the warming sunshine Justin Hope possessed? Oh, for Pete's sake, she was a woman, not a tulip bulb. She was being absurd again.

Holly turned into a walkway and looked up at the big three-story house before her. The sign on the front door said in Old English script HOLLY'S BED AND BREAKFAST.

It was her childhood home, where she'd taken her first steps, spoken her first words, grown from child to girl to young woman. It was where she'd returned to—no, fled to—when her world had crashed down upon her and she was frightened and alone. She had come home. And she never intended to leave her safe haven again.

Such a pretty house, she mused, the color of a robin's egg, a delicate blue with the gingerbread trim pristine white. On the front porch was white wicker furniture with padded blue cushions and, hanging by chains, the bench swing she'd spent hours on as a young girl.

If the house could speak, Holly thought, it would tell stories of love and laughter, of a happy child wrapped in the warm cocoon of her parents' love. It would whisper sorrowfully of the death of Holly's mother, of a father and daughter clinging to each other for comfort. And it would tell of a Holly lost, and a Holly found, as she sought solace in the house when her world had crumbled.

Holly was pulled from her reverie as she heard a car approaching. Justin, she wondered. Well, if it was, she had no intention of him finding her waiting on the front walk like a welcoming committee of one.

She hurried up the three wide steps to the porch and entered the house. The front hall was dominated by the old-fashioned registration counter she'd discovered at an auction and refinished herself. The comfortably furnished living room was empty, so she headed for the kitchen. Her father and Melinda were in the large, cheerful room, busily shelling peas as they sat at the big oak table.

"Hi," Holly said, unable to keep from staring at Melinda. That wasn't Missy Hopkins, she was Melinda Hope, Justin's sister. Holly could see the resemblance now, the dark hair and blue eyes. And Melinda was as pretty as Justin was handsome. She was tall and slender, and looked every bit the eighteen years she'd claimed to be. Her hair fell in dark curls past her shoulders, and Holly wondered absently if Justin's hair began to curl when he needed a trim.

"Well, the plane crash victim returns," Holly's father said. Vern Richards was tall and lean, his hair thick and gray, and there was a smile always ready to light up his face. "How did it go?"

"I was dead," Holly said.

"I thought Charlie Potts said you could be wounded this year," Vern said.

"It's a long story." Holly glanced over her shoulder toward the front hall, then looked at Melinda again. "Mel . . . Missy, there's something you should know."

"What is it?" Melinda asked, looking up at Holly.

"When I was dead I met . . . that is, he thought I was hurt and tried to help me because he didn't know it was a drill. Charlie really needs to get a bigger sign and . . . oh, dear, I'm blithering."

"Indeed you are," Vern said. "What's wrong? Who did you meet when you were supposedly dead?"

"Justin Hope," Holly blurted out.

Melinda jumped to her feet, nearly tipping over her chair. "He's here? In Maple Tree? He found me? I stayed inside, Holly, so his detectives wouldn't see me. I won't go back to New York. I hate it there in that big, empty apartment. There's no one to talk to. No, no, I won't go."

"Oh, Missy . . . Melinda." Holly took the girl's hands in hers. "You have to see Justin, you know that. But if the two of you sat down and calmly discussed—"

"No," Melinda said, shaking her head. "He doesn't discuss, he dictates. Oh, Holly, can't you help me? Please?"

"What in the blue blazes is going on here?" Vern asked.

"Dad," Holly said, "Missy's real name is Melinda Hope. She's sixteen, not eighteen, and she ran away. Her brother, Justin, is here to—uh-oh. I just heard the bell at the desk."

"I won't let him take me back there," Melinda said frantically. "He doesn't understand how lonely

I am, how much I hate the way I have to live. I want to stay here with you."

Vern stood up. "Let's just calm down and take this one step at a time. The first order of business is to see who's at the desk. I'll go. You two stay here." He left the room.

Melinda's eyes filled with tears, and Holly tightened her hold on the girl's hands.

"Justin loves you, Melinda," she said softly. "He's been sick with worry ever since you ran away. He flew in from London when he heard you had been spotted in Maple Tree. I've talked to him, and I know how worried and hurt he's been by what you did. You have to understand, Melinda, that a part of him is angry too. He's worked very hard to provide the best for you, and he can't understand why you would do something like this to him in return."

Melinda sniffled. "That's just it, Holly, he doesn't understand me at all. I know Justin loves me, but he doesn't know me, not really. He was twenty and away at college when I was born. I was a surprise, but our parents were thrilled to have a new baby. Then when they . . ." She pressed her lips tightly together for a moment to gain control of her emotions. "They were killed in a boating accident two years ago, and Justin suddenly found himself in the role of father to me instead of just my big brother whom I rarely saw."

"It must have been a very difficult time for you both," Holly said.

"Justin tries to be a good father. He's even read books on parenting and all that junk, but . . . oh, Holly, he doesn't listen to me, hear what I'm trying to say to him. I don't want his money, I want to be with him. I want to talk with him, sit across the table from him at dinner, have him yell at me to pick up my room and turn down my stereo." A sob caught in her throat. "I want us to be a family."

"I understand," Holly said. "My mother died four years ago, and my dad and I reached out to each other and clung like Super Glue. Yes, I can see that you're lonely and need Justin's presence more than his checkbook. But you have to be fair too. Instant fatherhood couldn't have been easy for him. He honestly feels he's done what is best for you. You two are on opposite ends of the pole right now. The tricky part is to find a middle ground, a way to compromise."

"He won't listen to me," Melinda said, shaking her head. "I know he won't. He'll put on his corporation face and that will be that."

Holly laughed. "His corporation face?"

"Well, yeah," Melinda said, managing a small smile. "He doesn't show any feelings, just stares at you like you're a bug."

"I've seen his corporation face," Holly said, still smiling. "It's like a curtain falling into place."

"Exactly. He could probably make millions playing poker."

Vern reentered the kitchen. "Well, ladies, it took some smooth talking and considerable charm, but I've convinced Mr. Justin Hope to sit down in the living room and talk about this situation."

"You're kidding," Holly said.

"He's a tough man," Vern said, "but a decent human being. Melinda, your brother is at the end of his tether because of what you've put him through. Tread softly, young lady, or you're liable to get your bottom walloped. Well, go on, he's waiting for you."

"I don't want to talk to him alone," Melinda said, her eyes widening. "I always lose. Justin is used to dealing with corporate giants who know every trick in the book. I'll end up agreeing to something before I know what hit me. You've got to come with me, Holly. Please?"

"Me? Oh, no, Melinda. Believe me. I'm the last person you want in your corner. Justin is not overly fond of me and my interference in this as it is."

"I take it that you got mouthy?" Vern said, raising his eyebrows.

Holly rocked one hand back and forth. "So-so. Just a tad." She paused. "Well, maybe more than a tad." And then there was the matter of that kiss and the lingering, confusing effect it had had on her. No, she definitely did *not* want to confront Justin Hope at the moment.

"Ladies," Vern said, "Justin doesn't strike me as a man with an overabundance of patience. I did my part by getting him to agree to a powwow. I would suggest we get in there before my marvelous work is all for nothing."

"We?" Holly repeated.

"We'll go in force," Vern said, "then see how the chips fall. If Justin tosses you and me out on our backsides, Holly, we'll know he's going to insist on talking to Melinda alone. Come on. It's worth a try."

Holly sighed and shook her head, Melinda threw

up her hands, and the trio left the kitchen with Vern in the lead.

Like little piggies being led to the slaughter, Holly thought. She wasn't ready for this, did not want to see Justin. *He* might have a corporation face, a curtain he could drop over his features to hide his emotions, but *she* certainly didn't. Heaven only knew what he would see on her face. She was so confused, she had no idea which of her jumbled emotions might be mirrored in her eyes.

When the three entered the living room, Justin was staring out the front window, his back to the room. Melinda looked up at Vern, who nodded at her. She took a wobbly breath.

"Justin?" she said tentatively.

He turned slowly and Holly felt the increased tempo of her heart.

Such a magnificent man, she thought. Tall, dark, strong—forget that. He looked like a storm about to happen. That wasn't a corporation face, that was a mad-as-hell face. Oh, dear.

"Hello, Melinda," he said, his voice ominously low. "You're looking well. Being a runaway apparently agrees with you."

Oh, dear, dear, Holly thought. This was not getting off to a very auspicious start.

"Everyone sit down," Vern said.

"You've called a conference?" Justin asked dryly.

"We've grown very fond of Missy . . . Melinda," Vern said. "Holly and I are involved in this by our caring about your sister. I'm hoping you'll let us stay."

Justin shifted his gaze to Holly. "I see. Well, by

all means then, do join right in. You realize, of course, that Holly has already formed her opinion of the situation, and I didn't get many points in my favor."

"That's not true," Holly said. "I asked you to please slow down and you have." She sank onto a chair. "Melinda, sit."

Everyone sat, and a heavy silence fell over the room. Justin folded his arms across his chest and stared at Melinda, who stared at her hands, which were clutched tightly in her lap. Holly stared at Justin, and Vern stared at Holly. The seconds ticked by.

"This is ridiculous," Holly finally said. "Henry Kissinger never accomplished anything this way. Somebody has to say something."

"Fine," Justin said. "Melinda is coming home with me immediately."

"I am not!" Melinda said. "I won't go, Justin. I won't go back to that place and be alone and lonely. I'm staying here with Holly and Mr. Richards."

"I'm your legal guardian, miss," Justin said, "and I say you're going home."

"I'll run away again," Melinda said. "You're going to get very tired of coming to Maple Tree, Wisconsin, to get me. You'll make trip after trip to this town."

Interesting thought, Holly mused. Justin Hope popping into Maple Tree on a regular basis.

"Don't act bratty, young lady," Vern said.

"Amen to that," Justin said. "Melinda, go pack your things."

"Don't act pushy, young man," Vern said.

Oh, Lord, Holly thought. Her father was going to get his dead card.

"Now look here—" Justin started.

"No, son, you listen to me," Vern interrupted firmly. "The problems between you and Melinda aren't going to be solved by your telling her what to do. This calls for some good old-fashioned talking from the heart, and listening with the heart. I remember when Holly was sixteen. It was no picnic, believe me, but her mother and I did manage to survive."

"Thanks a lot," Holly said indignantly.

A hint of a smile touched Justin's lips. "Your Holly is still a handful to deal with," he said. *And she kisses like a dream.*

"Are you willing to talk things through, Melinda?" Vern asked.

"It won't do any good, but . . ." She shrugged. "Yes, all right."

"Justin?"

Justin narrowed his eyes and looked at Vern, then Melinda, then finally settled his gaze on Holly, who stared right back at him.

Again, silent seconds ticked by.

"Do you," Justin finally asked Holly, "have a room I can rent?"

"Excellent," Vern said. "Come on, Melinda, let's finish tending to those peas. Holly will get you registered and squared away, Justin." He hurried from the room with Melinda right on his heels.

Holly got slowly to her feet. "I'm glad you're staying, Justin," she said, meeting his gaze across the room.

His voice was low when he spoke. "Are you?" He rose and closed the distance between them.

"Well, yes, because . . ." she started, then stopped speaking to draw air into her lungs.

Why did she have such difficulty breathing when he was close to her, she asked herself. And why was there heat thrumming throughout her? And why did Justin have the most gorgeous blue eyes she'd ever seen? Why, why, why did he look so good and smell so good? Why did the memory of their kiss make her heart beat wildly?

"Because?" he repeated.

She blinked. "Because . . . um, dragging Melinda home without discussing what's troubling her won't solve anything. This is a much better plan."

"Well . . ." He drew one thumb lightly over her lips. Holly shivered. "We'll see what develops, won't we?"

Three

Fingers of sunlight danced across Justin's face, every bit as insistent as a puppy wanting to play. Justin groaned and turned his head in an attempt to escape from the intrusive nuisance. He slowly surfaced from the foggy depth of a deep sleep but refused to open his eyes.

The first order of business, he hazily decided, was to remember where he was. London? Paris? Switzerland? New York?

He shifted slightly on the bed and realized that beneath one of his hands was his belt buckle. His belt buckle? He'd slept with his pants on? Why in the hell would he do that?

He inched his hand upward to find his shirt, then went farther to what was obviously a night's growth of stubbly beard on his face.

Still not opening his eyes, Justin gathered his facts. He was very groggy but didn't have a hangover. He had, apparently, slept like the dead, and had done so fully clothed. But where was he? He would, he supposed, have to open his eyes and find out.

He tentatively opened one eye halfway, then closed it again as the bright sunlight attacked him with no mercy. He tried again, opening both eyes but squinting against the ruthless glare. He looked around the room, seeing an old-fashioned pitcher and bowl on the dark upright dresser, an easy chair upholstered in blue-and-white-striped material, and white eyelet curtains blowing gently in a breeze coming through the open window. The clock on the nightstand announced that it was eleven-fourteen.

Justin blinked, blinked again, and began to remember. He wasn't in London or Paris. He was in Maple Tree, Wisconsin. He'd found his sister. Melinda was here. And Holly. Ah, yes—delectable, maddening, confusing Holly Chambers. One minute he had been sharing a kiss with her, and in practically the next moment he'd been ready to wring her neck for telling him how to handle Melinda.

He was, he realized, in the room he'd rented at Holly's Bed and Breakfast. He'd stretched out on the inviting bed with the idea of relaxing for a few minutes, and it was now nearly noon of the next day.

He replayed in his mind the scene that had taken place the previous afternoon in the living room. He'd had every intention of standing his ground, of telling Melinda that her performance was over and he was taking her home. Even though Vern Richards had tried to ease the tension between brother and sister, and Melinda had looked sad, angry, and frightened, he had still been determined to return immediately to New York with his wayward sister in tow.

And then he'd looked at Holly.

Some strange emotion he couldn't identify even now had twisted within him as he'd gazed at her across that living room.

There she had sat, staring at him with those big, fawn eyes of hers, her blond curls in appealing disarray around her lovely face. Her lips had seemed to beckon to him, asking him to cover them again with his. He'd been momentarily mesmerized, and his firm stand to take Melinda and leave had been shot to hell. He'd heard himself asking to rent a room, which meant he'd agreed to discuss with Melinda whatever had prompted her childish stunt of running away.

"Damn that Holly Chambers," Justin said, sitting up and swinging his feet to the floor. "She's driving me nuts."

He found his suitcase next to the door and took out his shaving kit and clean clothes. The bathroom was at the end of the hall, he remembered, and he carried his bundle from the room.

In the shower Justin allowed the hot water to beat against his body and clear the last traces of sleep from his mind. Now, he vowed, he was back in control. He was *not* totally responsible for his actions yesterday, as he'd been numb with fatigue. Holly had *not* cast some eerie spell over him, despite his behavior to the contrary. She was *not* his type, with her tendency to view the

world as though it were one love story after another. The kiss had been nice, very nice, but it
had *not* been the earth-shattering experience his
tired body and brain had seemed to consider it at
the time.

Justin shaved in the shower, then stepped out
to dry with a large blue towel. Yes, he was definitely back in control. Holly Chambers was lovely
and had a fresh, wholesome quality to her. She in
no way resembled the sophisticated women he
dated, who considered marriage and babies ta-
boo. They knew the rules, played the game, a
good time was had by all, and no one got hurt.

Justin pulled on jeans and a navy-blue knit
shirt. When he went downstairs and saw Holly, he
would view her through the eyes of a man who'd
had the sleep he desperately needed. Holly was a
candidate for a cornflakes commercial, not for
sharing his bed. That he was still in Maple Tree
was due to his being a victim of jet lag, and had
nothing whatsoever to do with Holly Chambers.

Lord, it was good to be in command of himself
again.

Justin combed his hair, straightened the bathroom, then returned his shaving kit and rumpled
clothes to his room. He would, he thought as he
went down the stairs, have to sit down and talk to
Melinda about her so-called problems. He had
witnesses to the fact that he'd agreed to do that.
Besides, witnesses or not, Justin Hope always
kept his word.

So he'd listen to his sister, knowing full well
that sixteen-year-old girls blew things out of proportion. He'd read that in one of the books on

parenting. Yes, he'd listen, and then, by damn, he was taking Melinda back to New York where she belonged.

Justin glanced into the living room that was glowing with sunshine but was devoid of people. "Bed and breakfast," he supposed, meant that a person was on his own for lunch and dinner, and he'd slept long past the breakfast hour. But maybe there was a cup of coffee left in the kitchen. He never felt his day had really begun until he'd had his jolt of caffeine.

He pushed open the swinging kitchen door and stopped, half in and half out of the room. His heart thundered in his chest, and he felt a rush of heat low and fierce in his body.

He had one thought: Dammit!

Holly was standing at the counter, her back to him. She was wearing red shorts, red tennis shoes with no socks, and a red-and-white checked blouse. His gaze swept over her, the gentle slope of her hips, the enticing outline of her bottom in the snug shorts, and the satiny length of her legs. He missed no detail of her, and he frowned as he felt the ever-increasing response of his body.

This wasn't supposed to be happening, he told himself. He was back in control, had tucked Holly into the slot where she belonged, and chalked her off his list of things to worry about. So why did he have the almost unbearable urge to pull her into his arms and kiss her senseless? Why was he envisioning running his hands over those shapely legs, then inching his fingers beneath the shorts and—no, this absolutely was not supposed to be happening. Coffee. He needed a cup of coffee.

He came farther into the room and cleared his throat. Holly looked over her shoulder and smiled at him. He stifled the groan that would have revealed his reactions to her, and his frown deepened.

"Well, good morning," Holly said. "You certainly were tired. You look much better now." If he looked any better, she thought, she'd faint on her nose. Justin Hope in faded jeans was a sight to behold. Trim waist, narrow hips, muscled thighs pressing against the soft fabric. Yummy. And her stomach felt fluttery and strange. "There's coffee on the stove."

"Thanks," he said gruffly. He took a mug from a pegboard on the wall and filled it with the steaming liquid. "Where's Melinda?"

He turned from the stove just as Holly turned from the counter, and their eyes met across the length of the large, sunny room. Justin forgot about his coffee. Holly couldn't remember what he had just asked her. They were held immobile under the gaze of the other, unable to think, or hardly breathe. Heat churned within them, and that sensual current they'd felt the day before wove around them again, determined to draw them close, so close, together.

Justin was the first to move, shifting his attention to the mug in his hand. He took a sip of coffee, then looked at Holly again.

"Dammit, Holly Chambers," he said, his voice rough, "what are you doing to me?"

"I . . ." she started, but ran out of air. She took a deep breath and tried again. "Me? I'm not doing anything."

"Ha!" He glared at her, then strode to the table where he sat down and took another swallow of coffee.

"Ha?" Holly repeated.

"You heard me."

"Well, you're certainly grouchy for someone who got caught up on his sleep. I'm not sure what you're accusing me of doing, but whatever it is, I'm not doing it on purpose."

"I suppose those tight shorts were an accident. They just jumped out of your dresser drawer and landed on your body."

She peered down at her shorts, then looked at him again. "What's wrong with these shorts? They're perfectly ordinary cotton shorts from K mart."

"Ha!"

"Would you quit that? Besides, if I were one to get picky, which I'm not, I'd mention the fact that those jeans fit you like a second skin, but I won't. I could also ask you what you're doing to me, because you make my stomach feel funny, but I won't do that, either. I'm going to finish chopping my carrots and ignore you because you're crabby." She turned back to the counter, then sniffed indignantly for good measure.

Justin smiled. He had intended to continue frowning, to stay just as crabby as he damned well pleased, but he couldn't help smiling.

She was something, he thought. Feisty as hell, and so damn beautiful he was going out of his mind. He wanted her. He wanted to make love to Holly with a need so great, it was turning him inside out. This wasn't supposed to be happening, but it was, and he had no idea what he was going to do about it. Holly *didn't* know the rules, or play the game. She lived her happy life here in Maple Tree, Wisconsin, a world that was light-years from his own.

Oh, yes, he wanted Holly, but he couldn't have her, and that realization made him feel empty and alone. There was only one solution to his bizarre lack of control in regard to Holly. He had to get out of this town . . . fast.

"Where's Melinda?" he asked before draining his coffee mug.

Holly scooped up the carrots and put them in a Crockpot that sat on the counter. "She went fishing with my father." She set the cover of the Crockpot in place.

Justin's coffee mug hit the table with a bang. "Fishing! Melinda? She doesn't know anything about fishing." He paused. "Neither do I, for that matter. Our parents had a home in Westchester, outside of the city, then I moved Melinda to my apartment in Manhattan after they died. Why would she go fishing?"

"She wanted to try it," Holly said calmly, wiping off the counter. "My father will teach her, just as he taught me. He has endless patience." She crossed the room and poured herself a mug of coffee. "Besides," she went on, walking toward the table, "Melinda needed to get outside. She's hardly poked her nose out of the door since she came here." She sat down opposite Justin. "Every time I looked for her she was busy dusting, cleaning, what have you. Melinda has more than earned a day off."

"Dusting and cleaning?" Justin said, leaning toward Holly. "Melinda wouldn't know a dustcloth if it bit her."

"You're starting to sound like a parrot," Holly said, laughing. "You're repeating everything I'm saying. I assure you that Melinda has been a tremendous help to me. I've been teaching her how to cook too."

"Cook?"

"Definitely a parrot," she said, and took a swallow of coffee.

Justin sat back in his chair and crossed his arms over his chest, shaking his head. "Fishing, dusting, cleaning, cooking. Melinda Hope? History is being made here."

"Try this one on for size," Holly said. "They left at dawn, because my father always says the fish are biting better then."

Justin burst out laughing. "That caps it. I'm having that kid fingerprinted. I don't believe she's my sister at all."

"You have a wonderful laugh, Justin," Holly said softly. "So deep and rich, as though it's coming from way inside you, from your heart."

"Really?" he said, his smile disappearing as he met her gaze. "I don't laugh very often, now that I think about it." He looked at her for a long moment before he spoke again. "Once, when Melinda was about four or five, my mother talked me into dressing up like Santa Claus and coming to a Christmas party Melinda was having with her friends. I was great. I did about a hundred ho-ho-hos until my dad finally whispered at me to knock it off and give the kids their presents. I was really into my role by then. I ho-ho-hoed all the way out the door. I haven't thought about that in years. I really had a good time that day."

Holly smiled at him and an unfamiliar warmth seemed to tiptoe around her heart. "I bet you were a wonderful Santa Claus."

He nodded. "I was. I came back to the house later in my regular clothes, and Melinda climbed up onto my lap and told me how Santa had come. He laughed, she said, and he yelled 'ho-ho-ho' all the time. Her eyes were sparkling, and she had a great big smile on her face. I can remember thinking . . ." His voice trailed off.

"Thinking what?" Holly prodded gently, covering one of his hands with hers on top of the table.

He looked at their joined hands, then back up at her face. "Thinking what an incredible feeling it was to be able to bring so much joy to someone else's life by taking some time out and just giving it all I had. I . . . never mind. I'm probably not making any sense."

"You're making beautiful sense."

He turned his hand over and caught hers before she could pull it away. Slowly he stroked her palm with his thumb. A shiver danced along her spine, swirled, then landed deep within her, pulsing with the same maddening, tantalizing tempo as Justin's thumb on the sensitive skin of her palm.

"I don't know what made me think of that day I played Santa," he said, his voice husky as he continued to gaze directly into Holly's eyes.

"Maybe," she said breathlessly, "it's because you're stopping, taking time out again for the first time in many years. And maybe because this time-out is centered on Melinda, just as it was when you played Santa for her."

Justin nodded. "Maybe. But I didn't agree to this time-out."

"Sometimes those are the best kind, Justin. They just happen."

"With no warning."

"No warning."

"I don't think we're talking about Melinda anymore, or Santas who yell 'ho-ho-ho.' I think—" He stood and pulled Holly up, drawing her close to him. "That this conversation shifted somewhere to the subject of you and me."

"Yes, I think you're right."

"You happened to me, Holly Chambers," he said, lowering his head to hers, "with no warning."

His mouth melted over hers, and his tongue slipped between her lips. He pressed his hands against her back, nestling her to him. Her arms encircled his neck and she savored his taste, his fresh, soapy aroma, the feel of his muscled body. Her breasts were crushed to his hard chest in a sweet pain, and she met his tongue eagerly with her own. His hands slid lower, over the slope of her buttocks, and he spread his legs to move her tightly into the cradle of his hips. His manhood surged against her, aching and wanting.

She was awakening, Holly thought dreamily, awakening after the long sleep of winter. The cold, lonely winter was at last over because Justin was there. He was spring, and she was basking in the warmth of his sunshine. She could feel his arousal and was aware of her own as liquid heat surged throughout her. Oh, how she wanted to make love with this man, become one with him, with Justin.

No warning, Justin thought. Holly had happened to him with no warning. But what exactly *was* happening between them? It went beyond his raging desire to make love with her. Far beyond. Emotions were intertwined with his passion, strange, new emotions that he couldn't get a handle on.

Every time he gained control of his thoughts regarding Holly, labeled her as a silly romantic and not a woman who would fit into his world, she stripped away his rational thinking with her smile, or laughter, or her big brown eyes. Now he was kissing her again and he shouldn't be, and his control over his body was rapidly following the path of his control over his mind—into oblivion.

He lifted his head enough to draw air into his lungs, then trailed a ribbon of kisses along her neck. She tilted her head back, eyes closed, to give him access to the soft skin. Her knees trembled and she gripped Justin's shoulders, clinging to him for support.

"Holly," he murmured, "how long do people fish?"

"Depends on the people," she said, opening her eyes halfway, "and the fish."

"I want you," he said close to her lips. "Lord, how I want you. And you want me, I know you do."

"Yes."

"This is our time-out, Holly. It happened, whatever this is, with no warning. This time-out belongs to us, we both want it, deserve to have it before I take Melinda—" He stopped speaking.

Holly opened her eyes the rest of the way and drew a shuddering breath. "Before you take Melinda home? Leave? Go?" She dropped her hands from his shoulders and took a step back, forcing him to release his hold on her. "Well, yes, of course you're leaving. I know that. Time-outs are temporary. They're isolated incidents like playing Santa Claus for your little sister. They're memory makers, the time-outs, nice things to reflect back on when the mood strikes, or just totally forget, whichever suits you."

"Holly, making love with you would be very special, very important. Forget the time-out bit. It doesn't sound right anymore, doesn't apply to what we're talking about."

"Doesn't it?" she asked. "I think it does. You're in Maple Tree, Wisconsin, Justin. You don't belong here, you'll be leaving as soon as you possibly can. I can't make love with you, don't you see? You'll go, the spring will be over, and I'll be forced back into the winter chill."

He frowned. "The what?"

"Never mind," she said, shaking her head. "If I try to explain, I'll sound like a tulip bulb. Justin, I shouldn't have kissed you like that again. I led you to believe that I was willing to . . . I'm sorry. I'm not a tease, I swear it."

"I know that. I didn't intend to kiss you again, either, but it happened. Our wanting each other is happening too. Can you just walk away from that?"

"I have to. I don't know how to do time-out when it comes to making love. I wouldn't know how to deal with it, where to put the memories, the realization of what I had done after you were gone. I'm not a woman who can sleep casually with a man, Justin. There's been no one since my husband died. I'm twenty-six-years-old, and I've been a widow since I was twenty."

His eyes widened. "You haven't been with a man in six years? Six?"

"Six," she repeated. "I can't make love without being in love, and since I refuse to fall in love again, I haven't made love. Understand?"

"I guess so," he said, dragging a hand through his hair.

"I want you, Justin, more than I've ever wanted anyone, even Jimmy, my husband. We were so young, just children really, and we had only a year together. Now I'm a woman, and my desire for you is like nothing I've ever experienced before. But I can't do it, Justin. I can't make love with you because I don't love you."

But what if *he* was falling in love with *her*, he wondered. Oh, holy hell, what if *that* was what had been happening to him? If he fell in love with Holly Chambers, it would be, without a doubt, the dumbest thing he'd ever done in his entire life.

"You're angry at me," she said. "I can tell."

"What? Oh, no, no, I'm not angry. I know you're not a tease. I've got an ache in an obvious place, but I'm not angry. I understand and respect what you've just told me. You have to be in love to make love, and you aren't in love with me."

"No, I'm not. Thank goodness."

"Oh, well, thanks a lot," he said. "May I ask what would be so distasteful about being in love with me?"

"Not distasteful. Futile. I mean, really, Justin, think about it. You said yourself that you have no time for a serious relationship. You zip-a-dee-doo-dah all over the world, making important deals and probably wining and dining beautiful, so-phisticated women. We're from such different worlds, we might as well be on separate planets. You know all this, Justin."

Damn right, he did, he thought, and he'd do well to remember it. Holly was the wrong woman in the wrong place at most definitely the wrong time.

"I have work to do," she said. "There's no point in continuing this conversation, anyway."

"Hold it," he said, raising a hand. "One question. You said that you refuse to fall in love again. Why?"

She stared at the toes of her tennis shoes. "I'd rather not discuss that part. It's a very private matter between me and me." She looked up at him again. "It's been lovely kissing you, Justin, but I have to tell you that I don't intend to do it again. There's the bell at the desk." She scooted around him. " 'Bye."

He turned and watched her leave the room. "It's been lovely kissing me?" He shook his head. No one had ever said *that* to him before.

He ran one hand down his face, then began to pace the floor. He had to get a grip on himself, he decided firmly. He was Justin Hope, for crying out loud. He walked in and took charge in boardrooms across the globe, commanded and received maximum effort from the finest staff of employees, had the final say on decisions involving millions of dollars, and was responsible for the lives that money touched. He had power and authority, and gained respect wherever he went. He'd earned his way to the top by hard work and a reputation for honesty and intelligence. He was in control.

But not when it came to Holly Chambers.

Was he actually falling in love with her, he asked himself again. In love with fresh, natural, homespun Holly, who sighed happily whenever she saw romance taking place around her? Holly, who herself wanted no part of love?

Why, he wondered, continuing his trek back and forth across the kitchen. She'd been married for only a year before her husband died, and had admitted she'd been hardly more than a child then. What had happened to make Holly the woman vow never to love again? Why was she allowing one year out of her life to determine her entire future? So many questions. He wanted, and would have, the answers.

He wandered out of the kitchen and along the hall. Holly was coming down the stairs as he reached the registration desk.

"I just rented the last room," she said. "Holly's Bed and Breakfast is full at the moment. Six guests, including you and Melinda, plus Dad and me. The other guests are here to fish, and are always up and out at the crack of dawn."

Justin shoved his hands into his back pockets. "How long have you had this place?"

"I grew up in this house," she said, walking behind the counter. "When I left to marry Jimmy, my parents felt like they were rattling around in here. My father had retired from the postal service, and my mother from teaching grade school. They hated to give up this wonderful old house, and got the idea to open a bed and breakfast. They named it after me. When I . . . came back home, I helped them run it. Then when my mother died four years ago I took over her duties as well as my own, and my father and I continued on."

"I take it you like what you're doing," he said, looking at her intently.

"Oh, yes, very much, but even more, I like being in this house, in this town. I should never have left here, but I'm back and I don't intend to leave again. This is where I belong."

"I see." But he really didn't. Why was Holly clinging so tightly to the house and town where she grew up? "I need to make some business calls. I'll put all the charges on my credit card." He glanced at his watch. "Shoot, it's only about four in the morning in Tokyo."

"You can use the office. It's the door right behind the counter here. No one will disturb you in there." She paused. "Tokyo?"

"Yes, I have some holdings there. I hope I can at least get through to Paris. It's very important." He moved around the counter and opened the office door. "Holly?"

She turned to face him. "Yes?"

"There *is* a world beyond Maple Tree, Wisconsin, beyond this house."

"I know that, Justin, and it's very obvious that you've traveled in that world extensively," she said softly. "I ventured out there once and it was wrong for me, a terrible mistake that I won't ever repeat."

Her words puzzled him, but he nodded and went into the office. So many unanswered questions, he thought, with the biggest one at the top of the list in capital letters.

Was he falling in love with Holly?

Four

Holly spent the next hour preparing bran muffins for breakfast the following day. She would
serve them with eggs, bacon, and a huge bowl of
fresh sliced fruit.

Melinda, she mused, had been so excited at the
prospect of going fishing for the first time. Her
blue eyes had been sparkling, and her smile had
been genuine, making her look like any other
happy, bubbly sixteen-year-old about to embark
upon a new adventure. But Melinda wasn't happy.
She was miserable living in New York.

Holly sighed. She musn't interfere, she told herself. Justin had made it quite clear that he wasn't
asking for and didn't appreciate hearing her opinion on his relationship with his sister. But Holly
cared about Melinda, and hated to see the sad-
ness that settled over the teenager like a heavy,
dark cloud.

And Holly cared about Justin too.

She walked out into the hall and saw the office door was closed.

The business tycoon was still at it, she thought as she went out the front door. Justin was, no doubt, in his element, giving commands, wheeling and dealing, talking to people in Paris and Tokyo. That was Justin's arena, and with it came the glamorous women who could sleep with him, give him what he wanted, without falling in love with him and asking for a commitment he wouldn't make.

Holly sank onto the bench swing with another sigh. She was thoroughly depressing herself, she realized, setting the swing in motion. She shook her head, then filled her lungs with the fresh spring air. Spring, after the long sleep of winter. Awakening to sunshine and warmth after the lonely chill. Justin.

"No," she whispered. She had to stop this. She was content with her life just as it was. She was where she belonged, doing what she wished to do. Yes, all right, she *did* want to make love with Justin, join him in ecstasy. But she could not, would not, make love with a man she didn't love. And she wasn't in love with Justin Hope.

Was she?

Oh, how ridiculous, she admonished herself. How could she even ask herself such a dumb question? She hardly knew the man.

Still, he'd given her glimpses of his depths, of the man beneath the powerful, authoritative exterior. He'd lifted the curtain and shown her the caring part of him, a person who took time out to play Santa Claus for a little girl. A man who had yelled ho-ho-ho and treasured the sparkle in his sister's eyes.

What Holly didn't understand was why a man like Justin Hope had centered his attention on a woman like her. Not that there was anything wrong with her, of course. She was sort of pretty, in an Ivory-soap kind of way. She was intelligent enough to run a business and make a profit. She was a decent, caring human being who found genuine joy when she witnessed romance in bloom for those around her.

But she wasn't remotely close to being Justin's type of woman, and she knew it. Then why did he want to make love with her? Why was he so determined that she acknowledge that something unique and special was happening between them? Simply because she was there? Better than nothing while he was stuck in dull Maple Tree, Wisconsin?

She'd strangle him with her bare hands!

"Oh, Holly, shut up," she said aloud. It didn't matter what Justin's motives were. Justin himself didn't matter. Oh, darn it, yes, he did matter, far too much. Her greatest fear was that she'd been changed forever by meeting him. He'd come, he'd seen, but just how much of her had he conquered? She didn't know.

Well, great, Holly fumed, she *had* thoroughly depressed herself after all. She felt like having a long, loud cry, although she'd be hard put to explain why. Justin was beyond her reach, and she knew that. Even if she were willing to love again, Justin was the wrong man. She'd had enough of this nonsense. She wasn't going to think about Justin Hope for another second.

"Holly?"

Her head snapped around and she gasped as Justin stepped out onto the porch.

Oh, darn him, she thought, he was just so magnificent, so blatantly masculine from head to toe. There was an aura of virility emanating from him. And just to look at him was to remember even more vividly the feel of his lips on hers, his tongue dueling with hers, his arousal strong and full against her. Oh, why didn't he go take a nap!

"Did I startle you?" he asked, smiling.

And quit smiling. "Yes."

"I'm sorry. Thanks for the use of the phone."

She dragged her gaze to the cuff of her shorts and meticulously straightened the folded edge. "You're welcome."

"I think I'll take a walk downtown and get something to eat."

"Oh, yes, well, you must be starved," she said, still fiddling with the red material. "We serve only breakfast to guests, but you're welcome to help yourself to whatever is in the kitchen. I made stew for dinner."

"I'm not a guest?"

She shrugged. "Not exactly. I mean, Melinda eats with us, and you belong with Melinda, so . . . do whatever suits you, Justin."

He chuckled. "Whatever suits me?"

And don't chuckle that sexy chuckle. "About meals."

"Oh, about meals. I thought you were giving me an open ticket there for a minute." He paused. "Is there something wrong with your shorts?"

"My shorts?" She patted the cuffs. "Oh, no,

they're fine. Cute as a button, regulation cotton shorts. I like red shorts. They're perky."

Justin walked across the porch and settled next to her on the swing, stretching his long legs out in front of him and crossing them at the ankle.

And don't sit on my swing. "I thought you were hungry," she said, still not looking at him.

"I am, but I'm more concerned about what's wrong with you," he said quietly.

She met his gaze at last. "Wrong? Nothing's wrong. What could possibly be wrong?"

"That's what I'm waiting for you to tell me, Holly. You're about to jump out of those perky red shorts of yours. Talk to me."

"I really don't have anything to say."

He frowned. "In other words, you covered it all in the kitchen. It was lovely kissing me, but we're old news now, finished before we really had a chance."

Holly jumped to her feet, setting the swing to wobbling and knocking Justin off balance. He pushed himself up to tower over her.

"A chance to do what, Justin Hope?" she asked, glaring at him. "Hop in the sack together? Have a wham-bam-thank-you-ma'am to relieve your frustration and boredom while you're stuck in this hick town?"

He narrowed his eyes and his hands curled into tight fists at his sides. "Is that what you really believe?" he asked, a steely edge to his voice. "Do you think I've been playing games with you, amusing myself for the lack of something better to do? Did you do one of your fantasy mind trips and decide this was a farmer's-daughter scenario, and

I'm the hustling city slicker who's just passing through? You're slipping, Holly. That isn't even close to a romantic story. Dammit, have you dusted off what's happening between us as being unimportant?"

Holly stared up at Justin with wide eyes. Had she really just seen pain cross his face like a shadow, or had she imagined it? The anger was there, visible in the tight set of his jaw, the icy blue of his eyes, but there had been something else too. Pain? Oh, heavens, he was confusing her even more, making it impossible for her to think clearly.

She pressed her fingertips to her temples. "I —I just don't know what to believe. It's all so . . ."

"Confusing?" he said, his voice suddenly quiet and gentle. "Tell me about it. My brain turned into scrambled eggs when I realized—" *Whoa, Hope,* he told himself. This wasn't the time to tell her he might be falling in love with her. That's just what the city slicker would say to the farmer's daughter about now. "Hey, I'm sorry I yelled at you, okay?" He pulled her hands free and cradled them in his.

"I'm sorry too, Justin. It's not like me to hurl such nasty accusations at someone. It's just that . . . oh, I don't know what to say. I don't seem to behave very well around you."

He smiled at her. "You kiss very well around me." His smile faded. "Don't shut me out, Holly, don't hide behind a protective wall. Don't say it's been lovely kissing me but you don't intend to do it again. I want to kiss you, hold you, feel you respond to me."

She looked up at him suspiciously. "Why?"

Why? Because he needed answers, he thought. He had to know if he was in love with her. "Because—what kind of question is that?"

"A very reasonable one. I can't for the life of me figure out why a man like you would be interested in a woman like me. Not that there's anything wrong with me. I'm a very nice person. The fact does remain, however, that there are vast differences between us. Well, everyone knows that men and women are not anatomically the same, but I'm referring to differences in our basic life-styles, outlooks, the way we conduct our lives on a day-to-day basis. We're not remotely close to—"

He kissed her.

He did not, he had decided, want to hear a dissertation on why he and Holly weren't suited for each other. He knew how far apart their worlds and life-styles were without her spelling it out in a long, depressing list. He could tell her to be quiet, clamp his hand over her mouth, or—

He kissed her.

He wove his hands through her silky hair and pressed his mouth against hers. She was, at last, blissfully quiet. He drank of her sweetness, filled his senses with her feminine aroma, and refused to think beyond this moment.

Oh, Justin, don't, Holly thought in near panic. When he kissed her, she was lost. When he kissed her, she didn't care about anything but the hot sensations swirling through her and the glorious message that this was Justin, and his kiss was a gift-wrapped portion of heaven. When he kissed her, rational thought fled, and she gave way to her senses. When he kissed her, she wanted more, wanted to make love with Justin Hope.

"Yoo-hoo, Holly, are you—oh, good heavenly gracious me."

Holly and Justin jerked apart as though a bolt of lightning had sliced between them. Holly blinked, then registered the horrifying fact that Mrs. Hill was standing on the front walk, holding a wicker basket and staring at them with her mouth open.

"Hello, Mrs. Hill," Holly said weakly. "How . . . nice to see you."

"Yes, well, it's certainly interesting seeing you, dear," Mrs. Hill said, smiling sweetly. She looked at Justin. "I don't believe we've met, young man."

"Justin Hope. I'm a . . . very close friend of Holly's."

Mrs. Hill came up onto the porch. "Yes, I can see that. How delightful, just grand. We ladies in the church guild have often said that Holly should have a . . . close friend. Just because that Jimmy Chambers was a scoundrel doesn't mean that all men are worthless and—"

"Mrs. Hill, please," Holly said. "This isn't what you think. Justin and I were just . . . um . . . that is, we were simply . . ."

"Kissing the living daylights out of each other," Mrs. Hill said, beaming. "Why, it's a wonder you even heard me call your name. Oh, this is just marvelous. I've seen you glow when the little romance bug bites someone else, Holly Chambers. You're long overdue to have your turn."

"You're absolutely right," Justin said, flinging his arm around Holly's shoulders. He hauled her against his side with a thud. "That's exactly what happened. That little romance bugger just waltzed up and bit us both right in the—"

"Justin!" Holly said.

"Holly, dearest, my sweet patootie," he said, "you wouldn't want Mrs. Hill to tell the ladies of the church guild that you were kissing a stranger on your front porch just because he was handy, would you? Think of the rumors that would sweep through Maple Tree about your brazen behavior." He sighed dramatically. "No, my cupcake, it's better to confess that we have been bitten by the romance bug."

"Rumors?" Holly said, her mind racing. "Oh, good Lord." She started to pull away from Justin.

He tightened his hold on her. "Rumors. But since Mrs. Hill knows the truth, we don't have a thing to worry about. Right, Mrs. Hill?"

"Oh, absolutely," Mrs. Hill said, appearing extremely pleased with herself. "I'll set those wagging tongues straight, starting with Myrtle Sawyer across the street. I saw her peering from behind her curtains as I came down the sidewalk, but I couldn't imagine what she found so interesting. Well, I learned soon enough, didn't I? That Myrtle is a terrible gossip, just terrible, but I'll tend to her, don't you fear."

"Ohhh, I can't believe this," Holly said, squeezing her eyes closed.

Mrs. Hill patted her cheek. "Just leave this to me, honey."

"You're too kind, ma'am," Justin said solemnly. "Holly and I will be eternally grateful for your assistance and . . . oomph," he said as Holly's elbow jammed him in the ribs. "Whatever. Ow!"

Mrs. Hill shoved the wicker basket at Justin, who managed to snare the handle.

"That's an apple pie for your supper," Mrs. Hill said. "Vern loves my apple pie. I crumbled cheese on the top just the way he likes it. Now I must dash over to Myrtle's. There's just no telling who she's been on the phone to already. Ta-ta, children. I'm just so thrilled for you both." She hurried down the steps and a few moments later she was bustling across the street.

Justin peered into the basket. "Apple pie, huh? I wonder if Vern will share?"

Holly shook her head as though to clear it, flung Justin's arm off her shoulders, and found her voice. "Justin Hope, do you have any idea what you've done?" she asked, none too quietly.

"I certainly do," he said decisively. "I may live in New York, but the ways of small towns are not unknown to me. Maple Tree is a juicy rumor waiting to happen. These folks thrive on anything that will break the routine. Am I correct? Of course I am. What have I done? I've saved your reputation, Holly Chambers. But, hey, don't feel that you have to thank me. I'll reap my reward from the warm inner glow of knowing I've performed a humanitarian act on your behalf."

"Thank you?" Holly shrieked. "I'm going to murder you. Mrs. Hill and her cronies have a buddy system for spreading news. This will be all over town by nightfall, my sweet patootie."

"Holly, Holly," Justin said, shaking his head, "would you prefer that the rumor mill said that you were dallying with a stranger, behaving like a wanton woman?" Dallying? he repeated silently.

Wanton woman? He was laying it on a little thick there. Oh, well. "Would you?"

"No, but . . ."

"This is much better," he went on. "We've been bitten by the romance bug, remember? Who can find fault with that? Boy, this pie smells good. I'm so hungry, I'm about to pass out. I guess I'll go downtown and get something to eat."

"No," Holly said, pressing her hands against his chest. She quickly glanced around. "No, no, don't go downtown. People here are not shy, Justin. Once word gets out about us, they'll come right up to you and ask you to tell them all the details."

He shrugged. "I can handle it."

"No! Please don't go downtown. Eat that pie, all of it, or rummage around in the refrigerator and help yourself to whatever is there."

"If that's what you want me to do, cream puff, then I'll be happy to oblige. Your wish is my command."

"Would you stop that? It's really obnoxious."

"It's romantic, Holly. If anyone should realize that, you should. By the way, Mrs. Hill and Myrtle are both looking through the curtains now. It would appear, I'm sure, that you just can't keep your hands off my marvelous body."

Holly drew back from Justin's chest. "My life is out of control," she mumbled. "One minute I'm taking part in a perfectly normal plane crash, then . . . I can't believe this."

"Sweetheart, calm down." He kissed her on the tip of her nose. "Nice move, Hope. Myrtle will love that one. I've really got to get some food. Relax, dumplin', we're one step ahead of the enemy. My strategy is of a genius level."

"You are a very sick man."

"No, I'm a hungry man." He walked to the door. " 'Bye for now, my little dove."

"Oh, just put a cork in it, Hope," she yelled.

He laughed and went into the house.

Holly sank onto the bench swing, then rolled her eyes heavenward as she saw the curtains on Myrtle's window move.

This was a nightmare, she thought. She had been, until the arrival of Justin Hope, living a perfectly sane, ordinary, boring life. Then along came Justin and—

"Boring?" she said aloud. Had she actually thought that? Dear heaven, she had. Well, she was ignoring that slip in her mental gears because, after all, she was extremely shaken and stressed out at the moment. Boring? She wasn't bored, she was . . . serenely contented. There, that settled that. But then again . . . no, she refused to have this conversation with herself. She was going to save her energy for the nervous breakdown she was expecting to attack her at any moment. She just really couldn't believe this fiasco.

Justin settled at the table with a thick ham sandwich and a glass of milk. He'd put the wicker basket containing the delicious-smelling apple pie on the counter, deciding it belonged to Vern, and Justin would test the theory of "out of sight, out of mind."

He chuckled softly and took a bite of the sandwich. That had been quite a performance on the front porch, he mused. He felt like a man who had unexpectedly been dealt four aces. His sweet patootie Holly was going to have to play along with the love-bug number in order to protect her reputation. She was no doubt already concocting a story for the gossips of Maple Tree to explain why the romance of the year had fizzled out and Justin Hope had left town.

Well, he had news for Mrs. Chambers. He wasn't going anywhere, not for a while, at least. All the attention he would lavish on Holly, the smiles, the stolen kisses, would be very real. She'd have to cooperate, or blow what she thought was a charade. His ultimate goal was to chip away at the defenses she had built around her heart, then tell her all his actions had been sincere, that they owed it to themselves to discover what was truly happening between them.

Mrs. Chambers, he repeated silently. Mrs. Hill had said her husband Jimmy had been a scoundrel. What could he have done in the one year that they'd been married to make Holly vow never to love again?

Justin finished his lunch, put his dishes into the sink, then went out the back door to the large, neat-as-a-pin yard. He walked to the far end and leaned his shoulder against a huge tree.

Strange, he thought. He'd been so sure he'd provided Melinda with all that his sister could possibly want or need. Yet now, as he pictured packing his suitcases once again, kissing Melinda good-bye, and walking out the door, he felt a surge of guilt. What kind of brother left a young girl alone for weeks at a stretch, the opulence of her home supposedly making up for his absence? Especially after she had suffered the devastating blow of losing her parents. A lousy brother. But that's exactly what he'd done to Melinda in the two years since their parents had died.

"Damn," Justin muttered.

Melinda had been alone and lonely, and at last he understood.

It had taken his new and swiftly growing feelings for Holly to open doors in his mind, heart, and soul. He had grown and changed already since she came into his life. His tunnel vision had previously allowed him to see only Hope Enterprises clearly. The fleeting attention he paid to Melinda was an afterthought, an attempt to justify his negligence by giving her more money and taking her out nearly every night when he was home. But now, because of Holly Chambers, he saw the whole picture.

He'd been so damn wrong with Melinda, he realized. Big-time, strut-his-stuff Justin Hope had thoroughly blown it. Melinda had tried to tell him how she felt, but he hadn't listened, had dismissed her pleadings as adolescent dramatics. Heaven help him, he was a self-centered, full-of-his-own-importance rat.

A shudder ripped through him. He felt stripped bare, robbed of his control and power.

Easy, he told himself. Calm down. There was too much at stake here to allow himself to become totally rattled. The seemingly impossible business deals he'd put together around the world were child's play compared to what he was facing now.

What could he say, he wondered, to Melinda—and to Holly—to convince them that he had changed? Smooth talker that he supposedly was, he couldn't even begin to think of the right words.

But maybe . . .

Yes, maybe words weren't the answer. Actions were visible proof of intentions. He'd show them that he had come to his senses, now understood love on the plane of man to woman, and brother-father to sister-child.

Justin started back toward the house, aware that one image filled his mental vision, chasing away the dark shadows of loneliness.

Holly.

Five

Melinda burst into the kitchen. Holly jumped in surprise and nearly dropped the plate she was putting in the dishwasher.

"Oh, Holly, I'm sorry I slept so late," Melinda said. "I should have been up to help you serve breakfast to the guests."

Holly laughed. "You needed your rest. You were falling asleep in your stew last night. Your long day in the fresh air certainly caught up with you. Oh, by the way, your marvelous big fish is cleaned and in the freezer. That was a beauty of a catch, Miss Hope."

"I had so much fun. Your father said he'd take me fishing again whenever I wanted to go. But, oh, gosh, I should have been up to help with breakfast."

Holly snapped the dishwasher closed, turned the dial, and faced the young girl. "Breakfast went very smoothly, Melinda. All the guests are fed and on their way to wherever they're going today. My father kept their coffee cups full, I whipped up scrambled eggs to go with a bowl of fresh fruit and bran muffins and, my dear, your brother cooked bacon like a pro."

Melinda's eyes widened. "Justin? Justin cooked the bacon? My brother, Justin Hope?"

"The very same," Holly said, nodding. "He wrapped a towel around his waist and went to it. Every slice as crisp and straight as a pin."

"Awesome," Melinda said. "Really awesome. I didn't know Justin could fry bacon. Even more, I didn't know he'd even consider doing such a thing."

Holly shrugged. "He said he enjoyed himself. You know, Melinda, he was just as surprised when he heard you were dusting and cleaning, helping me as much as you are around here."

"I love doing this. We always had a housekeeper when my parents were alive, and Justin has one, too, so I never had a chance to touch anything. It's like living in a hotel. I like cleaning, setting things to rights, seeing everything look nice and knowing I helped do it." She paused, frowning. "Justin and I just found out something about each other that we didn't know before. That's kind of weird."

"No, that's a very good start. Did you ever stop to think that there is a lot more you two need to learn about each other?"

"Maybe. Where is Justin? I bet he's mad at me. Yeah, he's probably figuring I faked being tired last night and stayed in my room this morning so I could delay talking to him."

"Get some breakfast, Melinda," Holly said. "No, Justin is not angry. He said he was delighted you had a good time fishing. He sat on the front porch with me and my dad last night and chatted for a while, then went to bed." And neither Justin nor Holly had told Vern Richards about being caught in a clinch by Mrs. Hill. Her father would hear all about it from many sources soon enough. "Eat."

"Okay. Is Justin here?"

"No, he said it was such a beautiful day he was going for a walk before he closed himself up in the office with the telephone again. My dad has driven over to Pennington. That's a town about twenty-five miles from here. An old friend of his has a garage there, and he's the only one allowed to tinker with Dad's pickup truck. I don't expect him back for hours. When he gets to talking to his buddy, he loses track of time. Well, I'm off to strip beds."

"I'll help you."

"You'll eat breakfast, young lady. Then if you want to, you can take the stack of brochures on the front counter about the famous Holly's Bed and Breakfast downtown to the chamber of commerce. They called and said they'd given out the last one they had."

"Okay. Holly, did Justin say anything about me? You know, has he made up his mind that he's taking me back to New York, and we'll go on living just like before?"

"The subject never came up, Melinda. Justin promised to sit down and talk it all over with you, remember?"

"Go through the motions, you mean. He'll do

exactly what he wants to and I know it. He's never listened to me before. Why should this time be any different?"

"Did you ever think that Justin Hope would fry bacon for the guests in a bed and breakfast?" Holly asked, raising her eyebrows.

"No." Melinda laughed. "What an awesome scene."

"Life is full of surprises, Melinda. Don't decide how your talk with Justin is going to go before you've even had it. Now, eat your breakfast. Oh, and have a big glass of milk with it."

"Yes, Mother," Melinda said, smiling. "I promise to drink my milk."

Holly smiled and left the kitchen. Upstairs she entered Justin's bedroom and began to pull the sheets from the bed.

Mother, her mind echoed. Oh, how she'd dreamed of having a baby, Jimmy's baby, a child to care for, to love and watch over. But then . . . no, she wasn't going to dwell on that. Nothing was going to change the past.

She tossed the sheets into the hall, then returned to the bed and picked up the pillow, intending to remove the pillowcase. Instead, she wrapped her arms around the pillow and hugged it tightly to her, inhaling the aroma that was uniquely Justin.

She'd told Melinda that life was full of surprises. No joke, she thought. Justin Hope's emergence into her life had certainly been a surprise, but not an unpleasant one. Well, okay, she'd admit it. Justin was disturbing but wonderful. Dangerous but exciting. Sitting on the porch the previous night with Justin and her father, watching the fireflies dance in the darkness, had felt so right, so real, so very warm.

Another memory of Justin had been carefully tucked away in her heart, she knew. That was all she would have soon, just the memories. Justin would take Melinda and leave, and Holly would go on with her life as it had always been.

She sank onto the edge of the bed, still holding the pillow. No, she realized, that wasn't true. She wouldn't go on as she always had. Since meeting Justin, since being held and kissed by him, she was irrevocably changed. Because he had touched her life, she was never going to be the same again. And she knew without a single doubt that when he left, she would cry.

Why would the tears flow when he walked away? Why would her heart hurt, threaten to splinter into a million pieces? Why would she not allow the memories to surface until she was prepared to savor them without aching for Justin's presence?

The answers to the questions were hovering close, but Holly didn't want to face them. She just couldn't, wouldn't deal with the devastating truth. She didn't wish to see it in the glaring light of day for the futile, totally hopeless situation that it was.

But the truth was powerful, swirling within her, demanding attention.

"Go away," Holly said, shaking her head. "Go away and leave me alone."

The truth burst free, standing firmly before her, refusing to budge until she acknowledged it.

"Oh, damn," she whispered, a sob catching in her throat.

There it was. She was falling in love with Justin Hope.

"Damn, damn," she said as a single tear slid down her cheek.

She'd betrayed herself, broken the vow she'd made as she'd stood in the rain on that day so long ago and watched Jimmy's coffin being lowered into the ground. She would never love again, she'd promised herself, and for six years she'd held firm in her conviction.

Until Justin.

Inch by inch, breath by breath, kiss by kiss, and smile by smile, she was falling in love with Justin Hope. Oh, dear Lord, how had this happened? If only she could stop it, just turn off her mind and her heart, which hummed with joy at the mere thought of Justin. Justin, who would leave her.

Holly buried her face for a moment in the pillow, then lifted her chin and squared her shoulders. There was one saving grace to the dismal situation, she told herself. Justin would never know the depth of her feelings for him. She could at least salvage her pride, for he would never witness her tears of heartbreak when he left her and Maple Tree far behind forever.

"Lucky pillow," a deep voice said. "Where does a guy sign up to get a hug like that?"

"Justin," Holly said, gasping in surprise. "You keep sneaking up on me."

He crossed the room and hunkered down in front of her, resting his hands lightly on her knees.

"Are you all right?" he asked, studying her face. "You're awfully pale."

"Oh, I'm fine, fine. How was your walk?" She wished he would stand up, move away from her. All she had to do was lean over just a bit and her lips could capture his. The heat from his hands was spreading through her, igniting her desire. He had to move. Now. "Justin, would you please—"

"Kiss you? Ma'am, it will be my pleasure."

"No, I—oh!"

In one smooth, startling motion, he scooped her up and laid her full-length on the bed. The pillow was whisked away and replaced by half of Justin's body.

"Justin, for heaven's sake, the door is open."

"So is your mouth," he said, and covered it with his own.

This was totally disgraceful behavior, Holly told herself frantically. It was absolutely . . . wonderful. It was one hundred percent ecstasy. It was Justin.

She wrapped her arms around his neck and urged his mouth harder onto hers as she inched her fingers into his thick hair. She savored the taste and feel of him, and the passion he aroused in her.

A groan rumbled deep in Justin's chest as he drank of Holly's sweetness. Blood was pounding in his veins, and his heart was racing wildly. He wanted. He needed. He ached. Holly.

His passion-laden mind slowly remembered that the bedroom door was wide open. "Holly," he gasped, tearing his lips from hers. "Damn." He shifted off her, resting his weight on one forearm as he gazed at her flushed cheeks. "I want you so much," he said, his voice raspy.

Holly swallowed heavily. "Yes, well, I think it would be a good idea if you told me about your walk. Right? You bet. I also think we should move off of this bed."

"We'll compromise. I'll tell you about my walk, but we stay put."

"I really don't—"

"Holly," he said, looking directly into her eyes, "I saw so much while I was strolling along out there. There were flowers blooming and bright green grass that invited people to take off their shoes and wiggle their toes in it. The scents were so fresh, so good. It's all different from the concrete, glass, and steel of New York. New York always seems so colorless, just tones of gray, and a man's senses are assaulted by exhaust fumes and rotting garbage and a constant roar of noise. It's so peaceful here, so blissfully quiet. I like it, I really do. I've come to realize how long it's been since I've stopped working at maximum and really relaxed."

"Yes," Holly said softly, "I'm sure it's unbelievably different here from what you're used to."

"It's not just Maple Tree, Holly. Yes, I'm infatuated with this charming little town, but more important, I'm falling in love with you."

"What?" she whispered, her eyes widening.

"I've never felt like this before. Everything we share is special, rare. What is this if it isn't love? I really think I've found the answer to my questions. I think it's all adding up to my falling in love with you."

Oh, glory be, yes! Holly's heart sang. Justin was falling in love with her just as she was with him. Oh, yes, yes—no! "No," she said, shaking her head.

"I know our worlds seem to be poles apart, Holly, but I intend to change the way I—"

"Justin, please," she said, interrupting him, "listen to me. You said yourself that it's different here from anything you've known. It is peaceful, calm, slow-paced. It's offering you a change, and you're realizing you've been pushing yourself terribly hard for a long time. Everything looks wonderful to you, like a thirsty man in the desert coming across a muddy water hole. To him, it's the most beautiful water he's ever seen."

Justin frowned. "What's the point you're trying to make?"

"You're enjoying the change, and in the midst of it all, you found me. A small-town woman who doesn't put on airs or pretend to be something she's not. I'm sure I'm different, too, from what you're accustomed to."

"Holly . . ."

"Did it occur to you, Justin, that you're caught up in the moment? You needed, without realizing it, what Maple Tree offers you. Could it be that I'm part of the package? Part of the temporary escape from where you really belong? You'll leave here and go back to the life-style you're used to. That includes, I imagine, some very flashy, worldly women. Maple Tree, Wisconsin, as well as—as everyone here, will become nothing more than a dim memory." If only that weren't true. If only . . . "You know that's true."

He shook his head. "No. I don't believe it's true

at all. When I picture a future without you, I feel empty, cold. You fill me, make me complete, a whole man. You hold the keys to closed doors in my heart and mind. I'm not the same man I was when I came here, Holly, because you've touched my soul. If all of this sounds corny, I don't care because I mean every word. You're my raison d'être. I want you, yes, as a man desires a woman. But even more, I *need* you. Lord knows I'm no expert on the subject, but I honestly believe I'm falling very deeply in love with you."

"Oh, Justin, no. You and I can't—"

"Shh," he said, then really silenced her with a quick kiss. "Think about what I said, and believe me when I say I've changed a great deal since I've come to Maple Tree, since I've met you." He swung off the bed and started toward the door. "I'd better go before we get caught in here. Talk about juicy rumors." He stopped and looked back at her. "Yes, ma'am, I really do believe I'm falling in love with you, Holly. I like the way that sounds, and I sure like the way it feels." He turned again and strode from the room.

Holly struggled to sit up, then stared at the doorway through the mist of tears that filled her eyes. "I like the way it feels and sounds too, Justin," she whispered, "but it's wrong. It just isn't going to work."

With a sad sigh she slid off the bed and resumed her chores.

Hours later Holly and Melinda sat on the bench swing on the front porch, slowly moving the swing back and forth.

"You must be getting awfully far behind in your schoolwork," Holly said, breaking what had been a comfortable silence.

"No, I was way ahead. I was bored out of my mind in school. I'd finished the chapters in my textbooks and turned in oodles of extra credit. I'm really not missing anything."

"Oh, a whiz kid, huh?" Holly said, smiling.

"Well . . ." Melinda shrugged, then matched Holly's smile. "I'm not an airhead, that's for sure. I'm thinking about becoming a psychologist." She paused. "Is Justin still on the phone? The receiver is going to become permanently attached to his ear. Oh, look, there's Mr. Richards. He really did make a whole day of his outing. It's nearly dinnertime. Hi," she called to Vern as he got out of his truck.

Justin pushed open the screen door and joined them on the porch as Vern came up the steps.

"Fine thing," Vern said. "I go off for a few hours and what happens? Holly and Melinda get as lazy as old ladies, just sitting on the creaking swing doing nothing."

Justin chuckled.

"Ignore him, Melinda," Holly said. "That's my father's line when he's trying to draw attention away from the fact that he sat in a grimy garage all day shooting the bull. This is good training for a future psychologist, Melinda. It's reverse psychology on Vern Richards's part that isn't worth diddly."

Justin, Melinda, and Vern roared with laughter, then Justin's eyes met Holly's.

Time stopped.

The sound of Melinda's and Vern's laughter became a distant hum. The porch, the swing, the house, faded into oblivion. There was only Holly and Justin, drinking in the sight of each other, mentally reaching out to hold and touch and kiss.

I love you, Holly, Justin whispered in his mind. What else could this be if not love? Oh, yes, he loved her.

Oh, Justin, how I love you, Holly thought hazily. During the afternoon the *falling* in love had changed to *being* in love with him; she knew that now. It was still so futile, so wrong, such a terrible mistake, but it was too late to change it. She loved him, but he'd never, ever know.

"Yoo-hoo!"

Holly jumped, tearing her gaze from Justin's. "Oh, good grief, she scared me to death. I wish Mrs. Hill wouldn't yell so." Her eyes widened. "Mrs. Hill? Is she coming here?"

"She is indeed, my sweet patootie," Justin said. "Melinda, Vern, just go with the flow. Holly and I will explain later."

"Huh?" Melinda said.

Mrs. Hill bustled up the walkway and onto the porch. "Well, hello, all," she said, smiling brightly. "What a lovely family gathering. I understand you're Justin's sister," she said to Melinda.

"Yes, ma'am," Melinda said.

"You must be so thrilled about your brother and Holly," Mrs. Hill gushed on. "So, Vern? How do you feel about the romance bug biting your baby girl? Long overdue, wouldn't you say? Oh, they are such a fine, handsome couple."

"That they are," Vern said, nodding. "I couldn't

be happier. Holly and Justin are the perfect couple."

"We are?" Holly said, staring at her father.

Bless you, Vern, Justin thought.

"Aren't you?" Vern asked, all innocence as he looked at Holly.

"You bet we are," Justin said. He pulled Holly to her feet, holding her close to his side. "Right, my little pot pie?"

"Oh, yes, right," Holly said. "Pot pie?" she muttered.

"Huh?" Melinda said again, but no one paid any attention to her.

"Well, it's nearly supper hour, and I won't keep you," Mrs. Hill said. "I just wanted to drop by to assure you all that Myrtle and I have let the truth be known. There'll be no naughty rumors in Maple Tree. Not a one. It's been made clear that romance is in full bloom at Holly's Bed and Breakfast, and that Holly and Justin are so smitten they have trouble keeping their . . . eyes off each other. Everyone is just tickled pink as pudding."

"Ducky," Holly mumbled.

"That's great, Mrs. Hill," Justin said. "We appreciate your efforts on our behalf."

"Tickled pink as pudding?" Melinda said. "Weird."

"You're a fine woman, Gracie Hill," Vern said solemnly. "I do thank you for speaking up for the children. Oh, and the apple pie was delicious."

"My pleasure," Mrs. Hill said. "Actually, I thoroughly enjoyed telling everyone . . . I mean, I didn't mind sacrificing my valuable time to protect the reputation of this wonderful couple, and I'm glad you liked the pie. Well, I must dash. Have a lovely evening. Ta-ta for now."

" 'Bye," Holly said, waving one hand rather weakly in the air.

"What's going on here?" Melinda asked. "Gosh, I didn't realize Holly and Justin . . . how come no one tells me anything? I'm not a little kid, you know."

"You didn't go with the flow, Melinda," Justin said.

"I don't know what flow to go with. What's happening here?"

"A nightmare," Holly said, pulling out of Justin's embrace. She stomped across the porch. "Dinner is in ten minutes. If you're late, you don't eat." She flung open the screen door and went into the house.

"Uh-oh," Vern said. "Holly's upset."

"Well, so am I," Melinda said, getting to her feet. "I want to know what is—"

"Melinda," Justin interrupted quietly, "you and I will go for a walk after dinner, all right? I'll explain all this to you, and it's also time that we talked about other things too."

"Okay," Melinda whispered. "I guess."

"Let's wash up for dinner," Vern said, "and make it snappy. When Holly is in that kind of mood and says ten minutes, she doesn't mean ten and a half. I, for one, want some food."

"Go on in, Melinda," Justin said. "I need a minute with Vern."

" 'Kay," she said, and entered the house.

"Vern," Justin said, "I don't know how to say this except up front. I'm falling in love . . . no, in spite of the fact that I'm dumb as a post about this stuff, I know that I'm in love with Holly. I love her and I need her. I felt you had the right to know where I stand."

Vern studied Justin for a long moment, and Justin met his gaze directly.

"I see," Vern finally said. "Yes, I see it very clearly." A slow smile tugged onto his lips. "Son, I wish you well, I wish you luck, and I wish you the love of my little girl." His voice was suddenly choked with emotion. "Fight for her, Justin. Win her love, by damn, then return that love tenfold until you take your last breath. She's all I've got left now, my Holly. I'm trusting you with the most precious treasure on this earth. She may not know it yet, but she needs you too."

"Vern, I . . ." Justin swallowed heavily past the lump in his throat. "Thank you."

Vern nodded and the two fell silent. They had spoken man to man, father to son, and the new bond between them was solid and real. No more words were needed as they entered the house and went in search of Holly and dinner.

Due to Holly's stormy expression, dinner was quick, silent, and tense, with everyone more than relieved to push back their chairs and leave the table. Vern offered to help Holly clean the kitchen so that Justin and Melinda could go for their walk. Holly politely refused, saying she preferred to do the chore herself. Vern went to watch television, and Justin grabbed Melinda's hand and hauled her from the room.

"Definitely a nightmare," Holly said to no one, and began to clear the table.

Justin and Melinda strolled along Christmas Lane as the first vibrant colors of the spring sunset began to streak the darkening sky.

"So what you did with Holly in front of Mrs. Hill was a game," Melinda said, "roles you and Holly were playing because she caught you kissing on the porch. Am I getting this right?"

"Sort of," Justin said. "Melinda, I'm going to tell you something that Holly doesn't know yet. It's important that you don't let it slip that you know."

"You're trusting me with a secret?"

"Yes, I am. The most important secret of my entire life."

"Wow. Thanks, Justin. I mean, you know, for realizing I'm not some dumb kid who will spill the beans. That means a lot to me. What's the secret you're keeping from Holly?"

"Let's go sit on one of the benches in that little park over there."

"Is something wrong with Holly? Oh, Justin, tell me. Holly is special, and I like her so much."

"Come on."

When they were settled on the bench, Melinda immediately turned to look at Justin. "What is it?"

"Melinda, you grew up when I wasn't looking," Justin said quietly. "No, correct that. I just simply wasn't paying attention to you. When you ran away, I was worried sick, but I was also angry to

think you weren't satisfied with the supposedly
fantastic life I'd created for you."

"Justin—"

He raised a hand. "Let me finish, okay? Your
big brother is about to admit to his mistakes.
Hotshot Hope, business tycoon extraordinaire, was
a lousy big brother. It took coming here to Maple
Tree, slowing down and taking a good long look at
a lot of things, including myself, to make me realize I'd blown it. But most of all, it took meeting
Holly and—and falling in love with her, to turn
me around and start the changes within me that
are long overdue."

Melinda gaped at him. "You're in love? With
Holly?"

"I am. That's the secret I'm asking you to keep.
I haven't told Holly yet, because she isn't ready to
hear how deeply I care about her. She's vowed
never to love again because her husband was a
scum, although I don't know the details on that. I
do love her, Melinda, and I want to marry her. I
want the three of us to be a family, with hopefully
a couple of babies in the future."

"Oh, Justin," Melinda said, her eyes filling with
tears, "a family? Us? You're including me?"

"Of course I'm including you. There's no question about that. You'll never be alone and lonely
again. Melinda, since I met Holly I've come to
realize that I've been alone and lonely too. Your
brother may know how to make a lot of money,
but when it comes to people, special people, people I love, I'm a dud. Honey, I'm so damn sorry I
didn't listen to you, didn't hear what you were
saying to me. Things are going to be different, I

swear it. I don't expect you to automatically believe that, but I'll show you, prove it to you. Just give me some time, a chance. Will you do that?"

She flung her arms around his neck. "Yes, oh, yes. I love you, Justin. All I wanted was for us to be a family, be together. I don't need the money you give me. I want you there, that's all." She dropped her arms and dashed the tears from her cheeks. "Doesn't Holly love you, Justin?"

"I don't know," he said, raking a hand through his hair. "If she does, she's sure not telling me. She's fighting what's happening between us every inch of the way. She says she'll never love again, never leave Maple Tree. She's also convinced that she and I are from such different worlds, we'd never make it. Telling her that I'm going to change the way I live, the constant travel, all that, isn't enough. I have to do it, but that will take time. I have to put wheels in motion, delegate authority, revamp my business operations. I can set up a central control office anywhere I choose and work out of it."

"I understand."

"In the meantime, this town thinks Holly and I are romantically involved. I'm not playing a role when it comes to that."

"You really called her your sweet patootie? Justin, that's gross."

He chuckled. "I'm laying it on a bit thick, I admit, but it's keeping me close to Holly, and hopefully chipping away at the walls she's built around herself. When the time is right, I'm going to tell her how I feel and ask her to marry me. Marry us, actually. You're part of the package."

"I'm so happy, I could die, just die. Tell me what I can do to help."

"Don't let it slip to Holly about how I feel about her. I need time, Melinda. My business holdings are so spread out across the world and I may have to go to some of the places myself to get things squared away, but I'll postpone that as long as I can. In the meantime, you and I are staying right here in Maple Tree. I'll call your school in New York and see what needs to be done to have your work sent out here. Vern knows I love Holly, and I have his blessings. The rest is up to me."

"Oh, Justin, Holly will come to love you, I'm sure of it."

"I hope so." He paused. "God, she has to. I can't handle the thought of going through the rest of my life without her."

"We're going to be a wonderful family."

"Do you forgive me for being a rotten brother so far?"

"That's old news, forgotten. I wasn't such a ter-rific kid, either. Running away was a stinky shot to pull on you. I'm really sorry."

"Don't ever do it again," he said, smiling. "My old ticker couldn't stand the strain. But life has a way of working out, I guess. You ran away and found Holly for me. I owe you, kiddo. All I have to do now is convince the lady in question to fall in love with me, bury her ghosts, agree to marry me, and . . . oh, hell, what a list."

"You can do it, Justin, I know you can."

"I'll keep telling myself that."

"And I'll keep telling myself the sweet-patootie

bit is part of the number for Mrs. Hill. That is just so gross."

"Oh, I don't know, it grows on you after a while."

"Justin, really," Melinda said, rolling her eyes heavenward.

"No, huh?" He shrugged. "Oh, well. Melinda, do you think you could do one more thing for me?"

"Name it, it's yours."

"Well, I was thinking . . . that is, we could get up early tomorrow and . . . of course, if you don't want to . . ."

"Justin, what is it?"

"Melinda, would you teach me how to fish?"

Six

The next morning Holly began her spring cleaning with a vengeance. After serving breakfast to the guests and waving a breezy good-bye to Melinda and Justin, who were up at dawn to go fishing, Holly scrubbed the kitchen to within an inch of its life. Vern took one look at the tight set to her face, grabbed his fishing pole, and disappeared.

Holly cleaned and scoured, polished, rearranged furniture, and washed windows.

At dinner that night she looked somewhere over Justin's left shoulder, said it was a shame that Melinda had caught four fish to his none, then concentrated on eating her dinner. After tidying the kitchen, she pleaded exhaustion and went to her room.

On the front porch in the firefly-sprinkled darkness, Justin leaned his shoulder against the porch post.

"Holly's avoiding me," he said to no one in particular.

"Yep," Vern said.

"That's a good sign," Melinda said.

"Right," Justin said dryly. "I'm so thrilled, I can hardly stand it."

"Justin," Melinda said, "if you didn't mean anything to Holly, she wouldn't care if she was with you, away from you, or sitting on your lap. She's shook-up, probably confused, and just can't handle seeing much of you right now. Trust me. It's a good sign."

"Since when are you such an expert on the workings of a woman's mind?" Justin asked.

"My dear brother," she said indignantly, "I *am* a woman."

Vern chuckled softly. "Yep."

The next morning, after nearly being run over by the vacuum Holly was zooming down the hall, Justin ducked into the safety of the office and began to pace the floor, his dark brows knitted in deep concentration.

A Holly left alone to think, he deduced, could very well be a Holly coming to the conclusion that Justin Hope should be sent packing as quickly as possible. No way. He was going to make it clear to Ms. Scrub-and-Rub of Holly's Bed and Breakfast that he was very much on the scene and would not be dusted off, literally, that easily.

With a decisive nod Justin left the office and followed the noise of the vacuum. He entered the living room just as Holly turned off the cleaner and climbed up a three-step ladder set in front of the bookshelves. She teetered precariously on the top of the ladder as she began to dust.

His mouth set, Justin crossed the room. He clamped his large hands on her tiny waist and grinned at the enchanting view of her perky red shorts.

"Aak!" Holly yelled. She looked over her shoulder and glared down at him. "What do you think you're doing? Get your big paws off me, Justin Hope."

"Oh, no, ma'am," he said, smiling pleasantly. "My mother raised me to assist ladies in distress."

"I'm not! Go away."

"You're not what?" he asked, all innocence. "A lady? Or in distress?"

"I'm warning you, Justin."

"You're most definitely going to be in distress the way you're wobbling around up there. You just go right ahead with your dusting, and I'll hold you nice and steady. Pretend I'm not here." He flashed her a dazzling smile.

"Don't you have some tycoon-type stuff to do?" she asked, still glowering at him.

"Nope. Carry on with your chores."

Holly huffed noisily and turned back to the shelves. Oh, merciful saints, she thought, the heat from Justin's hands was incredible. It was swirling up from her waist to her breasts, making them ache for his soothing touch. And it was spiraling downward, landing and pulsing deep within her. Was he inching his fingers around over her stomach? Oh, good grief, he was, the rat.

Well, she'd be darned if she'd give him the satisfaction of knowing he was driving her insane.

She resumed her dusting, flicking the rag this way and that. She hummed a peppy tune and managed to bounce a bit in time to the rhythm, in spite of Justin's hold on her.

Justin stifled a groan as he riveted his gaze on Holly's bouncing bottom. His body tightened, and heated desire rocketed through him, causing a trickle of sweat to run down his back.

He was dying, he thought, and Holly Chambers knew exactly what she was doing to him, the little minx. She was giving him tit-for-tat, paying him back in spades for the way he was holding her. Lord, how he loved this woman. And if she didn't stop bouncing that delectable rear of hers in front of his nose, he was going to haul her off that ladder and—

"Done," Holly said. She shook the rag in the air, managing to toss a good portion of dust in Justin's direction. "Good-bye, Justin. I'm finished here."

He moved to the side of the ladder as he shifted his hands, and in the next instant Holly was lifted off and pressed against his body, her feet dangling above the floor.

"Put me down," she said, realizing immediately that her voice was shaky.

"Yes, ma'am."

Justin slowly slid her along the length of him. Every soft inch of her came in contact with every muscular inch of him, and her legs were trembling when her feet connected with the floor. Justin kept his hands on her waist, dipped his head, and claimed her mouth with his.

Oh, thank goodness, Holly thought.

The kiss was hungry, urgent, rough, and mutually shared. Tongues met and dueled. Holly's aching breasts were crushed to his hard chest as his arousal surged against her, announcing his want of her. The room seemed to disappear as wild passion consumed their senses.

"Justin, there's a telephone call for you," Melinda yelled from the distance.

He reluctantly raised his head, cleared his throat, and managed to respond. "Yeah, I'll be right there." He slid his tongue sensuously over Holly's lips. "It was nice dusting with you, Holly. I'll see you later." He released her and strode from the room.

Holly blinked, blinked again, drew air into her lungs, then sank onto the nearest chair. Oh, dear, she thought. Justin touched her and she melted. Justin kissed her and she dissolved. Oh, how she loved him, and, oh, how she wanted him, and, oh, dear, dear, what was she going to do?

With a rather bemused expression on her face, she tested her unsteady legs, decided they would support her, and proceeded to vacuum the living room, totally forgetting that she'd already done it.

To Holly, the day seemed endless. She continued to clean, and whenever Justin was free of the telephone, he popped up, sending her senses into overdrive and her heart to racing.

When she was straightening the kitchen cupboards, Justin decided he needed a glass of water and managed to trap her from behind between his body and the counter. Her breath caught in her throat as he nibbled on her ear before disappearing again.

When Holly crawled along the edge of the living room wall to wipe off the baseboards, she found herself nose to nose with Justin, who was coming from the opposite direction. He'd dropped a quarter, he claimed, and before declaring it lost forever, he kissed her until she couldn't breathe.

And so it went, with the sexual tension between them building until it was nearly palpable.

In the late afternoon Justin snapped at his New York secretary over the telephone, causing the woman to burst into tears. He apologized for ten minutes, while part of his mind and all of his body remained focused on Holly.

After dinner an emotionally and physically exhausted Holly beat a hasty retreat to her room.

Justin, Melinda, and Vern held their meeting in the darkness of the front porch.

"How long can she clean?" Justin asked. "I can't handle another day like this one."

"She washed the windows again today," Melinda said. "I think she's going to do everything twice."

"Wonderful," Justin muttered.

"There's a nice supper club in Pennington," Vern said quietly. "Good food, a dance band, highfalutin' place. A person might be convinced to get out of her scrubbing clothes and into a pretty dress if she was asked very nicely."

"Think so?" Justin said, hope ringing in his voice.

"Maybe, but maybe not," Vern said. "It's worth a try, though."

"Yep," Justin said.

Justin spent the next morning on the telephone. After eating a sandwich for lunch alone in the kitchen, he went in search of Holly. He found her on her hands and knees scrubbing the floor of the large pantry off the kitchen. He leaned against the doorjamb and watched the enticing wiggle of her jean-clad bottom as she scrubbed. It was several minutes before he spoke.

"Holly?"

"Oh," she gasped, nearly knocking over her pail of sudsy water. She turned her head to glare at Justin. "You scared me. I wish you'd quit doing that."

"Sorry. Having fun?"

"Oh, yes," she said, forcing a lightness to her voice as she started scrubbing again. "I love to get to the down-and-dirty of spring cleaning. It gives me a tremendous sense of accomplishment, excellence, a job well done."

"I see."

No, he didn't, Holly thought dismally. Justin couldn't see the jumbled messages in her mind, the loudest and most glaring of which was the announcement that she loved him. He couldn't see the tearstains on her pillow that came during the long nights she'd spent tossing and turning in her bed. Tears brought on by the knowledge that she was in love, hadn't meant to fall in love, but couldn't stop being in love, with Justin. He couldn't see that even now, with his vibrant presence seeming to fill the pantry to overflowing, that her body was throbbing with desire and she ached to fling herself into his arms. No, Justin couldn't see any of that. Thank goodness.

"It seems to me," he said, and she jumped again at the sound of his voice, "that great accomplishments, excellence, a job well done, should be rewarded."

She dropped the scrub brush into the pail with a splash, then turned to sit Indian-style on the floor, facing him. Her gaze skittered over his long, muscular legs, beautifully defined in faded jeans, then up across his broad chest and shoulders, which were emphasized by the clinging navy blue knit shirt he wore. Her heart beat rapidly, and she could feel the warm flush on her cheeks. She hoped Justin would attribute it to her nearly standing on her head to wash the floor. Slowly, reluctantly, she met his gaze.

"Rewarded?" she said. Oh, dandy, she thought. Her voice was trembling. Darn the man, she wished he'd take his gorgeous self out of her pantry. "Yes, well, maybe I'll treat myself to a long, leisurely bubble bath." She would be naked, waiting for Justin to open the door and come to her, slide his hands over her fragrant, soapy skin, then . . . "No, maybe that's not a good idea."

"It has possibilities," he said. Endless possibilities. "However, I was thinking of something else."

"Oh?"

Don't blow it, he told himself. Easy does it. "I was wondering, Mrs. Chambers, if you would do me the honor of accompanying me to dinner and dancing over in Pennington tonight?"

"Dinner and . . . over in . . . oh." She frowned. "Well, I don't . . ."

"Have other plans? Great. I'll make reservations and we'll leave here at seven. You'd better get back to scrubbing that floor before you lose all your bubbles. See ya." He beat a hasty retreat from the pantry.

"Hey!" she yelled. "I didn't say I'd go. . . ." She paused. "Dinner?" she mumbled. "Dancing? With Justin?" Not a smart thing to do. Very dumb, in fact. If her body and mind went nuts while she was sitting on a wet floor looking up at him, imagine what would happen if she was sitting across a table from him in a romantic, candlelit atmosphere. And imagine what would happen when he took her into his arms to dance to a slow, dreamy love song. Oh, mercy.

No, she wasn't going.

Absolutely, positively not.

She stared into space, then pressed one fingertip to her chin.

Should she wear her teal blue chiffon, or the raspberry-color sheath, or . . .

Justin entered the flower shop and smiled at the gray-haired woman behind the counter. He leaned one forearm on the counter and increased his smile to his best hundred-watt, knock-'em-dead dazzler.

"Hello," he said, "I'm Justin Hope."

"Oh, my dear boy, I know who you are," the

woman said. "You're Holly's young man. I'm Martha Sue Hartman, and I'm one of Gracie Hill's dearest friends."

Perfect, Justin thought. Got it in one. "Really? Mrs. Hill is a lovely woman, reminds me of my sweet departed grandma." He studied her for a moment. "So do you, as a matter of fact, Mrs. Hartman."

"Oh, what a darling thing to say. You just call me Martha Sue. We're all family in Maple Tree."

"What a comforting thought," he said, then sighed dramatically. "Yes, very comforting. It makes me feel as though I can confide in you, Mrs. . . . Martha Sue, just as I would have done with my grandma under these circumstances."

"Circumstances?" She leaned toward him. "What circumstances?"

Lord, Justin thought, in another minute Martha Sue was going to leap over the counter and pin him to the wall until he told her what was on his mind. "It's Holly," he said, then sighed again, deciding it had a very appropriate sound to it. He glanced around. "We are alone, aren't we, Martha Sue? I mean, this is a private matter."

She patted his hand. "Flowers have no ears, dear. Feel free to pour out your troubles to Martha Sue. What about Holly?"

"Well, we had a bit of a spat, you know what I mean? Nothing major, just a few cross words."

"What a shame. And?" She leaned over farther and crushed three chrysanthemums on the counter with her ample bosom.

Justin swallowed his chuckle and cleared his throat. "I feel just terrible that I snapped at Holly,

Martha Sue, just terrible. So tonight I'm taking her to dinner and dancing over in Pennington."

"Splendid," Martha Sue said, beaming.

"You think so?"

"Oh, my, yes."

"Good. I thought I'd bring her some flowers too. Roses, yellow roses."

"Excellent."

"Great. Tell me, Martha Sue, do you think that car I rented is a bit flashy?"

"Well, everyone in Maple Tree knows when you come and go because no one else has a red car with those fancy, shiny hubcaps, but it's not too flashy. I rather like it myself."

"Folks know when I come and go? So, I suppose, it will be common knowledge as to what time Holly and I leave for Pennington *and* what time we get back."

"Absolutely. That car has a rumbly engine, you know. There's not another like it in town. Older folks are light sleepers. Not me, of course, I haven't gotten to that age yet, but Gracie Hill will pop up in bed if a twig falls off a tree. She told me that herself. Why do you ask if folks will know what time you go and come from Pennington?"

"No reason, I'm just chatting," he said, whipping another big smile on her. *Hope, you diabolical devil, you.* This plan could definitely come under the headings of Rotten, Not Playing Fair, Cheating to the Max. Well, that was just too bad. If he didn't do *something*, Holly was liable to scrub that house until there wasn't any paint left on the walls. It was time for action. "May I have a dozen yellow roses, please?"

"I have only four. I don't have much call for roses in Maple Tree."

"Four it is, then. And thank you, Martha Sue, for hearing my woes. I can't tell you what this has done for my peace of mind."

"My dear boy, it was my pleasure. I'm just tickled pink as— "

"Pudding," he interjected.

"Yes, indeed, tickled pink as pudding that I could help. I'll get those flowers for you right now."

"Thank you, ma'am."

After two more thank-yous and another ear-to-ear smile, Justin left the shop with the four rather wilted yellow roses wrapped in green tissue. He stopped at the edge of the window and peered back into the store.

"Go for it, Martha Sue," he said under his breath.

He nearly cheered aloud when he saw Martha Sue snatch up the receiver to the telephone and dial as quickly as her chubby finger would allow. With a satisfied nod and a smug smile, Justin strolled away from what he now considered to be the scene of his brilliant crime.

"Justin," Melinda said, "those are the sickest flowers I've ever seen. Oops. Three petals just fell off."

Justin picked up the petals and tossed them in the kitchen wastebasket, along with the tissue-wrapped bouquet.

"Oh, well," he said, "they served their purpose."

"Holly never saw them."

"That's okay. Listen, I'm taking Holly to dinner and dancing over in Pennington tonight."

"Really? That's super, Justin. How did you convince her to go? She's been keeping clear of you lately, that's for sure. You turned on the suave Hope charm, huh?"

"Not exactly. I cut out before she could say no. Not classy, but I'm getting desperate." His performance at the flower shop had really lacked class, too, he thought. "I'd better get back on the phone. This change of command in my businesses is proving to be very difficult to handle by long distance. I need to go to some of those places, but I'm putting it off for as long as I can. The Paris office is in a mess at the moment and . . . well, I'll see how it goes. I don't want to leave Holly, not now. Things are too shaky. The ice I'm standing on is so thin I can see through it. I'll tell you something, Melinda. This being in love is complicated."

"But worth it?"

He smiled at her warmly. "Oh, yes, worth every minute. You'll find that out for yourself someday. I just hope it doesn't take you as long as it did me. I've wasted a lot of years being alone."

"And lonely," she said softly.

He nodded. "And lonely."

Hours later Holly sat on the edge of her bed wrapped in a towel. She'd showered and washed her hair, then blow-dried the blond curls into a soft halo around her face. Blanking her mind, not allowing an errant thought to wiggle into her brain space, she'd applied light makeup and her favorite floral cologne.

Now, as she sat on her bed, she was thinking. The thoughts she'd held at bay came tumbling forward, but she forced them to a screeching halt, making each wait its turn to be examined and tended to.

There were, she realized, really no new bulletins. The facts stood firm as they had since she'd first acknowledged them. She was in love, in love with the wrong man, and didn't want to be in love at all, no matter who the man might be.

But the man was Justin.

And the urgent business at hand, the matter that had to be dealt with immediately, was the evening ahead to be spent with him.

Holly folded her hands loosely together on her lap and stared at the far wall. Tonight, she realized with a sudden and strange inner calmness, was hers. Before her was the opportunity to have a romance more wonderful than any she'd imagined for her friends. She'd gotten great joy from fantasizing about future happiness for those around her, but tonight belonged to Holly Chambers.

Her romantic evening, she knew, wasn't real. Justin would be leaving Maple Tree soon, despite his saying that he thought he was falling in love with her. Then she'd have only memories. So, be it right or be it wrong, among those memories was going to be a Cinderella night of magic.

Was this fair to Justin, she wondered, then decided he wouldn't care. Once he left and returned to his world, he'd forget he'd even met her.

No, following the directives of her heart for one night wouldn't hurt Justin Hope. Her part in the romantic scenario would be honest, real, a woman in the company of the man she loved. The fantasy would come in the form of Justin, and the pretending that he returned her love.

Tonight was hers.

Dangerous, Holly asked herself. Probably. Should she fear that she was setting herself up for even greater pain, more tears that would be shed, a heart broken into a zillion, instead of a million, pieces? No. She wanted this night, was determined to have it, and would pay the piper later if need be.

Oh, yes, yes, yes, she thought, getting to her feet. Tonight was hers.

Justin restlessly paced the living room, glancing often at his watch. He was ready too early, he knew, and he was driving himself nuts. He was acting like an idiotic kid who was about to go to his first prom and who would prefer to go to the dentist instead. He was a wreck.

Melinda and Vern, the rats, had deserted the sinking ship of a nervous Justin and gone to an early movie. They would return soon to take care of preparing ahead some of the items for the next morning's breakfast. The four guests had come in a short time earlier, but hadn't stopped to chat. They were tired from fishing all day, they'd said, and were heading for bed so they could get an early start when the fish were biting in the morning. They'd all gone upstairs, leaving Justin to resume wearing his path in the carpet.

Justin looked at his watch again, then went to the bottom of the stairs, deciding he couldn't tolerate another minute in that living room.

"Good evening, Justin."

His head snapped up and he stared at the vision of loveliness at the top of the stairs. His heart thundered and his body tightened as heat coiled and churned deep and low within him. He couldn't speak, could only drink in the sight of Holly.

Dear Lord, how he loved her.

She was a gift from the sea, he thought. Her dress was neither green nor blue, but the color of the ocean waters. There was a filmy layer of sheer material over a darker one beneath it, and they changed shades as the light caught them. The dress emphasized her small waist, and the tops of her enticing beasts were revealed by the scoop neckline. Two narrow straps lay across her shoulders. She was exquisite.

"You're beautiful," he said, hearing the hoarseness in his voice. "A sea flower."

"Thank you, Justin," Holly said softly, then started down the stairs. And he looked magnificent, she thought. His tan herringbone sport coat fit well over his wide shoulders, and his dark brown slacks were obviously custom-tailored. He wore a tan and brown paisley tie against a pristine white shirt that accentuated his bronze skin and the night-darkness of his hair. Devastatingly handsome.

She continued down the stairs, feeling the heat

from Justin's smoldering gaze sweep through her like fire. Her skin was tingling, her heart racing. All her senses were sharper, missing nothing, memorizing all.

She reached the bottom of the stairs before him. The familiar currents of sensuality seemed to crackle through the air.

Without speaking, Justin framed her face in his hands and kissed her so softly, so sensuously, Holly's knees trembled. He lifted his head and looked into her eyes for a long, heart-stopping moment before dropping his hands.

"Shall we go?" he asked quietly.

"Yes. I'm ready," she said. Ready for all this night would bring to her.

Because tonight was hers.

More than two hours later Justin told himself yet again to relax. His stern, silent directive accomplished nothing. He still felt as though his muscles were going to creak from the pressure of his coiled tension.

While they were waiting for their coffee and dessert, Holly announced that she was going to the powder room. Justin got to his feet to assist her with her chair, watched her walk away, then slouched back onto his own chair with a stifled groan.

Holly was driving him right out of his everlovin' mind! He'd been fully prepared for her to be skittish, wary, her defensive wall firmly in place. He had intended to move slowly with casual conversation, idle chitchat, do all and everything to put her at ease.

So what did he get? A smiling, relaxed Holly Chambers, whose eyes were sparkling and whose attention was riveted on him. She watched every move he made, listened to every word he said, often leaning slightly toward him in rapt attention, affording him further glimpses of her breasts, which glowed like ripe, luscious peaches in the candlelight. She'd remarked more than once on the romantic atmosphere of the restaurant, and said she was certainly looking forward to dancing a slow, dreamy waltz with him.

Justin had nearly leapt over the table and kissed her senseless.

He was so off kilter, he admitted dismally, it was a sin. He should be deliriously ecstatic over Holly's behavior, chalking up points for himself toward his goal of winning the love of his woman. But a niggling little voice in his mind, a sixth sense that had held him in good stead as he'd sat across the bargaining table from the barracudas of the business world, told him something wasn't quite right.

He crossed his arms over his chest and considered Holly's actions. To borrow Melinda's vocabulary, Holly was acting awesomely weird. Why would a woman who had avoided him like the plague for well over two days suddenly shift gears and act as though he were the center of her universe, the man she loved? It didn't make sense, not one damn bit. He was so rattled by Holly's performance that he hadn't tasted one bite of his dinner or—

He stiffened, dropping his hands to the table.

Performance! he thought. Performance? Holly? Honest, up-front, unsophisticated Holly Chambers was playing games, acting out a role. putting on a performance? Yes? No? He didn't know. But even more, if she was, then why? What was she up to? What did she hope to accomplish? What in the hell did it mean?

Well, now, Justin thought, smiling as he drummed his fingers on the table, this was an interesting theory. Confusing as hell, but very interesting. So far, all he'd gotten out of the evening was a tension headache and a strung-out libido. To quote himself, he'd now go with the flow, follow Holly's lead, and maybe figure out what she was doing. Performance? He'd find out soon enough.

Lord, Holly was a complicated woman.

And he loved her more with every passing second.

Holly checked her appearance in the mirror that covered one entire wall of the sitting area in the powder room.

She looked lovely, she decided. There was a glow to her skin, a sparkle in her eyes. Oh, she was having a wonderful time, her Cinderella evening. It would help her secret scenario immensely if her Prince Charming were a tad more relaxed, but she wouldn't be picky about the situation.

She was, she knew, being herself, holding nothing back. She was in love with Justin, and she was acting like a woman in love. She adored watching him, so she watched him, memorizing his every nuance. His rich, rumbly voice flowed over her like warm honey, and she listened intently to every word he spoke, learning his opinions on the important and the mundane. The candlelight flickered over his bronze skin, and she drank in the sight of his handsome face at every opportunity. Heavens, she couldn't even remember what her dinner had tasted like.

Holly frowned slightly at she started toward the door. While she was having a fabulous evening, she now realized that Justin was not enjoying himself. She'd caught him more than once studying her as though he wished he could peer into her mind.

She'd satisfied her conscience on the matter of whether or not Justin could be hurt by her lowering her defenses for this one evening. She had decided he didn't have strong enough feelings for her for it to matter in the long run.

What she hadn't taken into consideration was that her sudden about-face in attitude and actions might confuse the poor man. Especially since she'd practically kept her head submerged in a scrub bucket for the past couple of days to avoid him. No wonder Justin was so tense. He was probably trying to figure out if she'd had a brain transplant.

Well, he'd live, she decided, leaving the powder room. Confusion was certainly not as painful as a broken heart, and to tell Justin that she loved him, that what he was witnessing tonight was real, would guarantee her a broken heart as well as the loss of her last ounce of pride. Justin was simply going to have to remain confused.

Because tonight belonged to Holly.

•   •   •

Justin watched as Holly made her way across the large room to their table. He saw the appreciative glances she received from other men in the crowded restaurant, and a strong surge of possessiveness flowed through him, the urge to yell to the others that Holly was his, and would be his forever.

He stood as she came closer, his gaze never leaving her. She smiled at him warmly, and, he decided, seductively.

He assisted her with her chair, but instead of immediately returning to his own, he leaned farther over once she was settled. He slid his hands down her arms and spoke close to her ear in a deep, low voice.

"I missed you while you were gone."

Holly's eyes widened, and she stared straight ahead. "You did?" she asked, her voice unsteady.

"I did. Your dessert is here." He dropped a light kiss on her bare shoulder. "I know what I'd like for dessert much more than that cheesecake waiting for me."

"Oh, good Lord," she whispered, her back ramrod stiff.

Justin straightened and stroked the back of her neck. He felt the shiver that coursed through her and, satisfied, returned to his chair. Holly, he saw, appeared rather shell-shocked.

"We'll go into the other room and dance," he said pleasantly, "as soon as we're finished here." He took a bite of cheesecake. "Delicious. Don't you want your strawberry pie?"

Holly blinked. "What? Oh, yes, of course. I adore strawberry pie." She shoveled in a bite.

"Are you all right, Holly?" He leaned toward her. "You seem suddenly . . . I don't know . . . jumpy, nervous." He raised his eyebrows questioningly, his expression oozing innocent concern. "Is anything wrong?"

"No, no," she said quickly. "I'm fine, just dandy."

"Good." He moved back and took another bite of dessert. He swallowed the cheesecake and smiled at Holly. A slow, lazy smile. "I'm glad you're fine and dandy. After all, the night is still young."

The night, Holly thought frantically, had suddenly slipped out of her control. Justin Hope no longer appeared tense or confused. Not by a long shot. He now gave the impression of being very much in command.

He also looked like he was about to toss aside that cheesecake and gobble her up for dessert.

Oh, good heavens, she thought in near panic, what had she done?

Seven

Beside the dining area of the restaurant was a large room with a polished wood floor, perfect for dancing. Chandeliers hung from the ceiling, their shimmering lights casting a soft glow over the gleaming floor and small tables. A band was set up on a raised platform, and was playing a waltz when Holly and Justin entered. Many couples were swaying to the music.

"Very nice," Justin said.

"Yes," Holly said. And very romantic, she thought. Custom-ordered for Cinderella. The only problem, she mused, was that Cinderella was now a nervous wreck because Justin Hope was suddenly behaving like the prince.

"Shall we snare a table first?" he asked.

"Yes," she said, then shivered as Justin slid his arm across her shoulders and pulled her to his side. She had to calm down, she told herself. Think! Something had happened to Justin while she'd been in the powder room. Did that mean she should change her actions and attitude too? Should she scurry back behind her emotional wall of defense, protect her fragile heart against what he would say and do?

Justin flipped a card on the top of one of the tables to the side that read Occupied, then smiled at Holly.

"May I have this dance?" he asked.

"Yes." Good grief, she sounded like a robot that had been set on automatic yes. She had only seconds left to decide what to do before Justin took her into his arms. Darn it, Holly Chambers, think!

He led her around the tables toward the dance floor, getting closer, and closer, and—

No, Holly decided suddenly, she wasn't running. Not from Justin, this Cinderella night, or from her own feelings. Justin could react anyway he chose, and she'd handle it, deal with whatever happened. She refused to be robbed of this one evening with the man she loved, behaving as the woman who loved him. Let Justin think what he would. This night was hers.

Closer to the dance floor . . .

Oh, help, Holly thought. No, she was fine, she was . . .

She was in Justin's arms, being pressed to the length of his firm body. She was inhaling his special aroma, feeling his heat that crept inside her, curling, swirling, pulsing low within her. She was wrapping one arm around his neck, pressing her breasts to his chest, and moving against him and with him in time to the seductive music. She was held safely, tightly, in Justin's embrace, and she didn't want him to let her go, ever.

Oh, yes, Holly thought dreamily, she was fine, more than fine. Here, in Justin's arms, was exactly where she wished to be.

She rested her head on his shoulder, nestled her entire body closer to his, and sighed. It was a contented sigh, an it-feels-so-good-to-be-home sigh, a womanly sigh. She welcomed the desire growing within her. She was in love with Justin—heart, mind, soul, and a body that throbbed to become one with him. Oh, yes, yes, yes.

Justin gritted his teeth and willed his body to stay under his control and command. He curled Holly's hand within his own and brought their entwined hands to his chest. Directives to his feet kept them moving in time to the slow melody. The sweet fragrance of Holly's hair and her cologne filled his head, and he swallowed a groan as she wiggled tighter against his aching body. He decided if he was going to die from the effect she was having on him, it was, at least, a fantastic way to go.

She felt good, he thought, and smelled good, and he wanted her with a burning hunger like none he'd felt before. His arousal, which was not following the commands of his mind, was straining against the front of his slacks. Holly had to realize what she was doing to him, but she was making no attempt to pull away. Why? Why was she behaving like this tonight, giving him signals that she wanted him as much as he did her? Why, after more than two days of hiding out from him?

Was it a performance, he wondered. A devious plan on her part to tease him to the limit, then call a halt? No, Holly wouldn't do that, not Holly. Would she? Was she so angry at him for pursuing her, for kissing her at every opportunity, and causing the Maple Tree gossips to talk about them that she'd decided to seek revenge? No, Holly wasn't like that. He just couldn't, wouldn't, believe it of her.

The song ended and another started, just as slow and dreamy as the first. All the couples on the floor appeared lost in their own worlds, not noticing anything around them. Holly and Justin danced on. Time lost meaning.

Suddenly Justin pulled Holly even closer to him to avoid bumping into another couple. Holly's eyes shot open as she realized just how aroused Justin actually was. She'd known he wanted her but . . . yes, she wanted him too. Forget Cinderella, who had run away from the prince at midnight. She was Holly Chambers, in love with Justin Hope, and she wasn't running anywhere, not tonight. She hadn't known how far her heart would take her during these magical hours, but now the truth was very evident to her.

She wanted Justin as much as he did her. She wanted to make love with him, be one with him. She wasn't frightened or appalled at her own raging desire, nor would she deny what she knew to be true.

"Holly," Justin said quietly, "can you feel what you're doing to me?"

"Yes."

"You'd better move a little away from me. I can't handle too much more of this."

She eased back from him so she could tip her

head up and look at him as they continued to sway with the music.

"Justin," she whispered, "I want you too. Tonight, this night, is ours."

Justin's heart thundered so violently, he was convinced everyone in the room could hear it. He gazed at Holly's face, her eyes, searching for some clue to what she was really thinking, but saw only a desire that matched his own. He quieted his doubts but couldn't erase completely the nagging questions in his mind.

"Are you sure?" he asked, still looking at her intently.

"Very sure. There's a small lake near here where my father and I used to go fishing. I discovered a marvelous stand of trees that hide a little grassy chamber. It's so lovely there. It could be our magical room, Justin, just for tonight, if you wanted to go there."

He nodded. Deciding he had gained enough control of his aching body to leave the restaurant without embarrassing himself, he led Holly from the dance floor.

Lord, how he wanted her, he thought. He could discern nothing on her face, in her eyes, in what she said, to indicate she felt any differently than he. Was it really true? Had he won the love of the woman he loved? He wasn't completely sure. Something bothered him about the way she kept referring to "tonight," as though it had no connection to the tomorrows. The little voice in his mind was still niggling at him, nudging him with warnings of alarm that something wasn't quite right.

Outside, the spring air was warm and filled

with the aroma of sweet wildflowers. The sky was an umbrella of silvery stars. They drove away from the restaurant, and the only words spoken were Holly's quiet directions to the lake.

How calm she felt, Holly marveled to herself. The desire within her was accompanied by a sense of peace, that all things were right and as they should be. It was difficult to fathom that she might regret the momentous step she was about to take. No, it was *impossible* to imagine ever being sorry that she'd made love with Justin.

"You can park here," she said finally.

Justin shut off the ignition, then folded his arms across the top of the steering wheel. He turned his head to look at Holly, seeing her beautiful face clearly in the glow of the stars.

"Tell me about Jimmy," he said in a low voice.

"Jimmy?" Holly said, surprised. "Why? He has nothing to do with tonight."

"I think he does. He's unfinished business, Holly. It's as though he's here, with us. Maybe I'm crazy to break the mood like this, but it's important. What did Jimmy do to you to make you so determined to close yourself away in Maple Tree? Please, Holly, I need to know."

She looked at him for a long moment, then nodded. "Yes," she said softly, "I suppose you have that right." She drew a shuddering breath. "Jimmy was simply . . . Jimmy. He was young, cocky, very good-looking, and he had a motorcycle that was his pride and joy. He showed up in Maple Tree out of the blue and went to work as a mechanic. Everybody was talking about him. He could be so charming, so endearing; he won everyone over.

He singled me out as his girl, and I was swept off my feet. Jimmy Chambers had picked me above all the others."

"What did your parents say?"

"They were concerned but admitted they really couldn't find fault with Jimmy. There was just something about him that troubled them. I shrugged it off as overly protective parents and went around with my head in the clouds. Finally Jimmy said he wanted to marry me, leave Maple Tree, and go live in a big city, where it was more exciting."

"And you agreed?"

"Not at first. I was sure that I loved him, but he wanted to elope, just run off, and I hated to hurt my parents like that. I kept stalling him, but he got impatient and said he was leaving and I'd better make up my mind if I was going with him."

"And you went."

Holly nodded. "I went. I kept telling myself how much I loved him, that my parents would understand, and I snuck out in the middle of the night to meet him. Off we went on that motorcycle. I left everything behind and ran away with Jimmy to Green Bay. We were married, and I got a job as a salesclerk in a drugstore. Jimmy worked in a garage."

"Then?"

"It was wonderful at first. My parents were upset, but accepted what I'd done. Two months later Jimmy said we were moving to Milwaukee. I didn't want to go. I'd been fixing up our little apartment, making it special for us, and I didn't understand why we couldn't stay there. Again Jimmy said he was leaving, and I could come with him or not, he didn't care. I was so hurt, and I began to realize he wasn't as sweet and wonderful as I'd thought he was. I went with him, but I knew deep within me that Jimmy really didn't love me."

"I see," Justin said, his jaw tightening.

"My life became a nightmare. We would just get settled somewhere and Jimmy would announce we were leaving. He started staying out late, then sometimes wouldn't come home for two or three days. I was lonely and miserable. I tried to tell him I needed stability in my life, but he wouldn't listen. My pride wouldn't allow me to tell my parents how unhappy I was. I wrote glowing letters, saying it was an exciting adventure to be on the go, that everything was fine."

"Don't you think your parents knew the truth?"

"They said later that they couldn't believe I was happy living like that, but I was a married woman, I'd made my choice, and they didn't interfere. Don't you see, Justin, I made the choice, and it was a terrible mistake. I loved Jimmy, and he was so wrong for me. Over the months, my love for him died and I felt empty, hollow, like a shell. Then . . ." Her voice trailed off.

"Then?"

"I found out I was pregnant. I was ecstatic, so sure that Jimmy would realize that as a father he had to settle down, give us a chance to be a family, start over fresh. I waited for him to come home that night so I could tell him about the baby. He didn't come. He couldn't because the police were chasing him. It had all caught up with him, all of it. He'd been stealing from the places where he worked, breaking into other businesses at night. When the police started asking him questions, we'd move to another town. That night they put it all together and came after him. Jimmy tried to outrun them on his motorcycle, but he skidded off the road and hit a tree. He was killed instantly. For some reason the police believed me when I said I hadn't known what he had been doing."

"And your parents? What did they do when Jimmy was killed?"

"They came to me, were there for the funeral. The three of us stood in the rain and watched Jimmy be buried. Just the three of us, me, my mother, and Dad. I vowed on that day that I would never love again, that listening to my heart was wrong. I would never run that kind of risk again. A week later I had a miscarriage."

"Oh, God," Justin said, shaking his head.

Tears misted Holly's eyes. "I came home to Maple Tree, to the house, the home, where I belonged. Everyone in town knew what Jimmy had done, but they were very kind to me. I kept the name Chambers to remind myself that I wasn't capable of choosing well when it came to love."

"You were just a kid then, Holly. You're a woman now, older, wiser. You can't let what happened back then dictate the rest of your life."

The tears spilled onto Holly's cheeks. "How do I know I'm wiser? I don't. The years went by and I didn't feel any more secure in my ability to fall in love with the right man. How was I to know whether I'd repeat my mistake? I couldn't take the chance. Then you came to Maple Tree and . . ." She shook her head.

Justin cradled her face in his hands, stroking away her tears with his thumbs. "And?"

And she'd fallen in love with him, Holly thought dismally. She'd once again fallen in love with the wrong man. A man of another world and life-style. A man who would leave her soon.

"What about me, Holly?" he asked gently. "What about us?"

"There is no 'us,' Justin."

"Then why are we here at this lake? Why were you willing to make love with me? Why, Holly, unless you're in love with me?"

"No. No."

He gripped her shoulders. "I think you do love me. I think you love me as much as I love you, and I do love you, Holly, with all that I am. I also believe that you're convinced that once again you've chosen the wrong man to love. Right? It makes sense now, your emphasis on 'tonight.' You weren't putting on a performance, you were stealing a night for yourself. You were going to have it all, on this night, then run back behind your wall in the light of the new day. I've figured it out, haven't I? Answer me, Holly."

"Yes!" she cried. "Congratulations, Mr. Hope, for being so astute, so clever. Yes, damn you, Justin, I love you, and you are as wrong for me in your own way as Jimmy was in his. I know that; I can't change that. But I was going to have this night, this one night, of allowing myself to act like a woman in love. One night of making love with the man of my heart. None of this could hurt you because I knew you didn't care that much about me."

"Not care? Didn't you hear what I just said? I love you." He shook her a little. "I am very much in love with you, Holly Richards Chambers."

"No, don't say that. I don't want to hear those words. It doesn't matter how I feel about you, or you feel about me. It doesn't matter one bit, because we're wrong together, Justin. We don't match. Our worlds are so different. You're going to leave Maple Tree, but I won't, not ever. Oh, it's hopeless. I just wanted one night of beautiful memories before you went away, and now I'm not even going to have that. Take me home, Justin."

"No. We don't match? We're totally wrong together? Then how do you explain this?"

He claimed her mouth in a harsh, punishing kiss that spoke of his frustration and simmering anger. His tongue delved deep into her mouth to find hers, and he pulled her roughly to him.

Somewhere in his mind, Justin's little voice changed from a whisper to a shout. This was Holly and he might be hurting her. Holly had said she loved him, and now he was going to destroy everything.

He wrapped his arms around her as though she were made of delicate china and gentled the kiss. His tongue stroked hers rhythmically, like the slow waltz they'd danced to. His lips were coaxing, sensuous, and she began to relax in his embrace.

He lifted his head. "Let's go to that private, grassy chamber of yours. We have to talk. I can't take you home yet with so much unsettled between us. That's all we'll do, just talk."

"There's nothing else to say," she said, breathless from the searing kiss. "Talking won't change—"

"Shh. Please?"

She sighed. "All right."

They walked the short distance to the lake, Holly tiptoeing to keep the heels of her shoes from sinking into the ground.

"Why don't you take off your shoes?" Justin asked, catching her arm to stop her.

"I'll snag my panty hose."

"Oh. Well, I'll turn my back, and you take off your panty hose."

"This is silly," she said, but quickly wiggled out of her panty hose when he turned around. She stuffed them in one shoe, picked up the pair, and poked him in the back with her finger. "All set."

"I'll follow you," Justin said. Anywhere, he thought. It sounded corny, but he meant it. He'd insisted on having this talk, but now realized he wasn't sure what to say to her. She was hiding behind her wall again, and it was tougher and stronger than he'd anticipated.

What Jimmy Chambers had done to Holly had definitely had far-reaching, damaging effects on her. Jimmy hadn't been just an irresponsible young man who'd hurt his teenage bride. He'd been evil, calculating, not remotely close to who and what Holly had believed him to be. He had been horribly wrong for her, but how was Justin to convince her that he, Justin Hope, was very, very right?

He followed her through a grove of trees, and they emerged in a clearing that was about ten feet long and twelve feet wide. The trees closed around them like a door shutting out the world. The grass was thick and soft, and silvery light filtered through the new leaves to cast an ethereal glow over the small area.

"This is my private place," Holly said quietly.

Justin pulled off his tie, then shrugged out of his jacket and spread it on the ground.

"Sit on that," he said, "so you don't get grass stains on your dress."

Prince Charming would have done something like that, Holly thought, sitting down. No, Justin wasn't Prince Charming, and she wasn't Cinderella. That was a fairy tale. This was real, heartbreakingly real, with no miraculous happy ending.

Justin settled on the grass next to her. "You're so beautiful in the moonlight," he said, looking at her.

She stretched her legs out straight in front of her, resting her weight on one hand. Fiddling with her skirt with her free hand, she kept her eyes averted from Justin's.

"Holly," he went on, "you said you love me, and I won't pretend that you didn't. I love you, too, and together there's nothing we can't solve if we put our minds to it. I'm very sorry about what you suffered because of Jimmy. But, Holly, I'm not Jimmy, and you're not the child who thought she loved him. This is now, this is us, and we could be so damn good together. But you have to give us a chance, or we're defeated before we hardly begin."

Holly kept toying with her dress. Justin frowned as he realized she wasn't going to reply, and a trickle of sweat ran down his back.

"I know you think our life-styles are completely different," he continued, "but I'm working on that. I'm delegating authority to more of my executives so I won't have to travel all the time. We could be a family, you, me, Melinda, and the children you and I would create. Holly, I love you, and I'm asking you to marry me."

She jerked her head around and stared at him with wide eyes.

That got her attention, Justin thought dryly. "I mean it. Will you marry me? We'll work everything out, I promise you."

"No," she whispered. "I can't marry you."

He gripped her shoulders. "Yes, you can. You love me, I love you. I'm changing my life so I can be with you. There's nothing standing in our way, Holly, except the past, and it doesn't have the right to dictate our future. Bury the painful memories, let them turn into dust. What's important is this moment, and every moment from here on."

"This moment," she echoed. "Yes, this moment is very important."

"And the tomorrows too. Don't you see that?"

She raised her arms to entwine them around his neck. "Can't we just have this moment, Justin?"

"No. You've got to look further than now. You've got to believe in me, trust me when I say that we'll have a wonderful, happy future together."

She leaned forward and outlined his lips with the tip of her tongue. A shudder tore through him, and he grasped her waist.

"Holly, don't," he said, his voice raspy. "You're not listening to me. Yes, this moment is important" —she pulled her arms free and began to unbutton his shirt. He sucked in his breath—"but it's not enough. You've got to promise me that you'll . . ." Her hands slid over his bare chest, her fingers teasing the curly dark hair. "Dammit, Holly. Promise you'll think about what I said."

"I'm thinking, Justin," she said in a husky, seductive voice. "I'm thinking that I want you to make love to me, here, in this lovely place, our private paradise." She pulled his shirt free of his pants and gazed raptly at his broad chest. "You're so beautiful, Justin."

Tonight was hers, she repeated silently. She was actually trying to seduce this man. She didn't want to dwell on tomorrow, or the day after that. This was now, and it was hers. Justin was hers.

He was *not*, Justin told himself, going to touch her until she promised to think about their future together. He wanted her so badly he ached, but he needed to hear her say she would listen, really listen, to him, give them a chance to have more than just this night. What she was doing to his body was heaven and hell, but he'd stay in control, wait her out, force her to think beyond the moment.

She pressed light, nibbling kisses over his chest.

Oh, good Lord above, he thought, a groan rumbling in his throat. His unsophisticated, nearly innocent Holly was ripping him to shreds. *Control.*

"Holly," he said in a hoarse whisper. "I'm dying. Tell me you'll think about our future, about marrying me. Say you'll—"

His words were cut off by her lips covering his, and her tongue slipping into his mouth to seek and find his.

He was lost. The fragile hold he had on his control snapped. The passion he'd been barely able to subdue burst into a raging flame, consuming him. He returned Holly's kiss hungrily as he lowered her to the ground. Any rational thought in his mind was forgotten. He ached, he burned, he wanted Holly with an intensity like none he'd ever known before. And tonight she would be his.

Oh, Justin, yes, Holly's heart sang. This was right, and good, and real. This was the time, the precious moment that was theirs alone. The world had stopped. There was no past, no future, only now. Oh, how she loved him. Tonight he would be hers.

Justin tore his mouth from hers and kissed his way to her breasts. They had been tantalizing him since she'd come down the stairs in that dress. He slid his tongue across the top of one, savoring the taste and feel of her dewy skin. His hand lifted to one of the tiny straps of the dress, then he hesitated, looking deep into her dark eyes.

Holly saw the question in his eyes.

"Yes," she whispered.

Hope, think! Justin's little voice shouted. Holly wanted only this night. He wanted all the tomorrows with her, a future until death parted them. If he made love with her tonight, would he destroy all hope of her looking forward and leaving the past behind? Or would she realize that they were meant to be, their lovemaking sealing a bond of forever?

"Justin? Please?"

"Holly," he said with a groan, "I don't know what to do. I want you so badly I ache, but I'm afraid that you'll—"

She placed one fingertip on his lips to quiet him, then moved away from him to sit up. Reaching behind her, she unzipped the dress, then slipped the straps down her arms. The filmy material fell to her waist, revealing her bare breasts. Starlight poured over her. She lay back down and smiled at Justin.

"You are so lovely," he said, his voice hoarse with passion. "Oh, Holly, I love you so much." His hand shaking, he cupped one of her breasts, stroking the nipple with his thumb, teasing it to a taut button. "Beautiful."

He leaned over and kissed her deeply, then his lips moved to where his thumb had tantalized her sensitive flesh. He drew the sweet bounty into his mouth, sucking, laving with his tongue.

At the feel of Justin's mouth on her breast, desire rushed through Holly, pooling low in her body. The rhythm of his sucking was matched by a pulsing deep within her. A soft purr of pleasure whispered from her throat. She pushed his shirt aside, wanting to see and touch all of him.

Justin lifted his head, understanding what she wanted. He unbuttoned his cuffs and pulled the shirt off. Her gaze flickered over his shoulders, his strong arms, the muscled contours of his broad chest, with the dark, curly hair gleaming in the moonlight.

"You're magnificent," she whispered. "I want you, Justin, more than I can tell you."

He gripped her dress, bunched at her waist, and skimmed it away with the lingerie beneath. She was naked in the silvery waterfall of glowing light, and his heart thundered. Without speaking, he stood and shed his clothes, feeling Holly's gaze on him. He was fully aroused, and when he lay down next to her, he placed one hand on her cheek.

"It's been so long for you," he said. "I don't want to hurt you, Holly, but I might because . . . damn, I just don't want to hurt you."

"You won't." She pressed her hands against his chest, then slowly moved them down. Lower and lower. "You won't."

Justin placed his hand on her stomach, then he, too, moved lower. They touched and caressed, explored the mysteries of each other. Their breathing was labored, their skin moist, their hearts racing. There was nothing too bold, no secrets kept but one, until they could bear no more.

"Oh, Justin, please," Holly said, a near-sob escaping her lips.

He moved over her and kissed her deeply, then gazed into her eyes.

"I love you, Holly."

"I love you too, Justin."

He entered her slowly, watching her face for the slightest flicker of pain. His muscles trembled from forced restraint as he waited for her body to adjust to him, to accept and welcome all that he brought to her.

She lifted her hips.

He filled her completely, sheathing himself in her heated darkness.

They were one.

He began to move within her and she matched his slowly rocking tempo. Her hands slid to his tight buttocks to urge him on. His rhythm increased. Faster, harder, wild and wonderful.

Holly gloried in the sensations rocketing through

her. She was alive like never before as she met Justin's pounding hips beat for beat. Tension gathered deep within her, coiling, twisting, tightening. She gripped his arms to keep from being lost as she was flung into an abyss of ecstasy.

"Justin!"

He drove within her one last time, then shudders racked his body. He groaned in pure male pleasure, then collapsed against her, burying his face in her neck.

She wrapped her arms around his glistening back and held him tightly to her, savoring his weight and musky scent. She closed her eyes for a moment, memorizing all that had transpired between them.

With his last ounce of energy Justin rolled onto his back, taking her with him, their bodies still joined.

"You were incredible," he said. "Did I hurt you?"

"No. Oh, no, it was beautiful."

"Yes."

They lay quietly, sated, their bodies cooling. Neither of them could have verbalized the contentment, the completeness they felt, but no words were needed. Holly nestled her head on Justin's shoulder and her eyes drifted close. Justin held her in his arms, her slender body stretched out on top of him.

He wasn't going to move for ten years, he thought. He'd never felt like this, not ever. Such . . . it had been . . . no, he couldn't find the words in his mind to describe the beauty of his lovemaking with Holly. He loved her, she loved him, and that had changed an act of pleasure to one so rare and precious, he was in awe of his own feelings. Holly was his now. And he had no intention of ever letting her go.

He closed his eyes and allowed himself to hover in the hazy place between being awake and asleep. He'd move in twenty years, he thought, smiling. He was in no rush to leave this heaven.

An owl hooted and Justin's eyes flew open. He blinked foggily, then realized he must have dozed off. Holly was asleep, her head still cradled on his shoulder.

How long had he slept, he wondered. He'd have to lift his arm to see his watch, and he didn't want to disturb Holly's peaceful slumber. She felt so good lying against him.

He brushed his lips over her forehead. Her skin was soft, he mused, like the petals of a rose, or a—

Suddenly he stiffened. Rose petals? Roses. The flower shop. Martha Sue and—"Holly," he said, patting her on the back. He looked at his watch and groaned. "Holly, wake up."

"Hmm?"

"Holly, listen to me. It's three in the morning."

She slowly lifted her head. "It's what in the who?"

He gripped her waist and gently lifted her off him. He reached for her dress and pushed it at her.

"Justin?" she said, shaking her head slightly.

"It's me, all right." He got to his feet and began to drag on his clothes. "Mr. Wonderful. It's three

A.M., Holly, and nice guy that I am, I made sure that the gossips of Maple Tree knew we were going to Pennington. They'll also know when we get back because of the sound of my car. Dammit, it seemed like a good idea at the time. Evil, but clever. I'm sorry, Holly, I really am."

She stood and began to dress. "You've lost me somewhere. You made certain everyone knew we were going to Pennington? Why did you do that?"

He stuffed his shirt into his pants. "I was desperate. You'd been hiding out from me, not letting me near you. I didn't give you a chance to refuse my invitation to dinner, then took care of having the word spread that we were going out together. I figured we'd get back around midnight, maybe a little later, and to Mrs. Hill and crew that would be racy stuff. If you continued to ignore me, they'd have a field day speculating about what happened between us. You'd have no choice but to be my sweet patootie again, and they'd decide all was well in romance land. If I was near you, I had a helluva lot better chance to chip away at your defenses. But, oh, brother, it's three in the morning! I really blew this."

"Oh," Holly said, zipping her dress.

"Oh? Could you elaborate a bit? Give me a clue as to how angry you are? I just shot your reputation to hell, in case you didn't notice."

She shrugged. *"C'est la vie."*

"That's life? Don't you understand what I've done?"

"Justin, believe me, our coming and going would have been common knowledge whether you implemented your rotten plan or not. I knew that when I left Maple Tree with you, and when I suggested we stop here. The whole town is going to know we didn't get back until nearly dawn, and tongues will wag. But that would have happened whether you'd told anyone of our plans or not."

"Then why did you do it?" he asked, raking a hand through his hair. "Why didn't you insist we head back right after dinner, or at least after a couple of dances? Being my sweet patootie is one thing, but now . . . Lord."

"I don't care what they say, Justin," Holly said quietly. "I honestly don't care. I wanted this night, was determined to have it. Whatever consequences I may suffer because of it will be worth it. The gossips can't rob me of my beautiful memories of these hours. No one can. The memories are mine. Tonight was mine." She picked up her shoes. "Let's go home." She turned and started through the trees.

Her words echoed in his mind. Was that all Holly wanted from this night, memories? What about the tomorrows, their future together?

Dammit, what about him?

Eight

After driving about five miles, Justin realized Holly was staring out the side window of the car and, apparently, had no intention of speaking to him.

What was she thinking, he wondered. Had she already withdrawn into her fantasy world of romantic scenarios, this one starring Holly Chambers and Justin Hope? Had she completely shut the door on any dreams of a future with him, and was now content to simply savor the memories of the night they'd just shared?

No! he fumed. She mustn't do that. They were in love with each other, had a lifetime of happiness and lovemaking waiting for them. He wouldn't let her slip away from him.

"Holly," he said quietly, "I'd like you to think about something." He paused, but she was silent. "You said that you would never love again because of Jimmy. Well, you *are* in love . . . with me."

Her head snapped around and she looked at him.

He glanced over at her, then redirected his attention to the road. "And I love you. You're a woman now, Holly, not the child who loved Jimmy. You left him behind a long time ago, and grew up. The woman you've become was ready, whether you realized it or not, to love again. And you did fall in love, and made love, and the past is behind you forever. Are you now going to deny that you love me?"

"No," she said softly. "I won't deny it. I do love you, Justin, very, very much."

Thank God, he thought.

"But," she continued, and a knot tightened in his stomach. "I also can't deny that I've once again chosen the wrong man to love."

"That's not true," he said, his voice rising. "Weren't you listening to what I told you earlier? I'm totally revamping my business, giving more authority to my executive officers. I'll have a central office to work out of, and my travel will be kept to a minimum. I want to be a husband, a father to Melinda, a father to the children you and I will have. What more can I do or say to prove to you that we *are* right for each other, that we have a wonderful future together just waiting for us to reach out and grab it?"

Oh, dear heaven, Holly thought, was it possible that she and Justin could have a future together? Their lovemaking had been so beautiful. Deep within her she had whispered the words of commitment to him, certain she would soon be alone with only her memories of him.

But Justin was speaking of forever, of changing his life-style, delegating his workload, cutting back on travel, concentrating on his family.

And he had said he loved her. His voice had rung with conviction when he'd declared his love, leaving no doubt in her mind that it was true.

But . . . she had to remember, she mustn't forget, once before she'd believed what she'd wanted to hear, and she'd been wrong. Once before she had acted impetuously and had paid a price she couldn't bear to pay again. Oh, it was all so confusing, so frightening, so . . .

"Holly? Are you listening to me?"

"Yes, Justin, I'm hearing what you're saying *now*, but what about who you really are, the man you were before you came to Maple Tree?"

"I've changed! Dammit, Holly, I think I began to change the moment I found you in that field and thought you were hurt."

"I was dead."

"Forget that. The point is, I'm not the same man I was when I came looking for Melinda. I've grown, recognized the mistakes I made with my sister, and fallen in love with a complicated, beautiful woman. I am in love with you, Holly Chambers, and love is powerful stuff. It's changed me a great deal. Why can't you believe that? Why can't you trust and believe in me?"

"Oh, Justin, I don't know if it's you I doubt, your ability to change your life-style so drastically, or if I doubt myself even more, simply don't trust my heart. It doesn't matter which doubt is stronger, because either way we don't have a future together."

"So you'll live off your memories." He shook his head. "Hell."

"You have your world, and I have mine. That's the way it is, even though I love you very much."

"No," he said tightly, "that is not the way it is, and I'm going to prove it to you. Words can't convince you? Okay, fine. Then you'll see actions. I've already spent hours on the phone starting the wheels in motion, and I'm going to continue revamping my business. I want the same world that you do, Holly, a home, family, security. It's just going to take a while so I can clear the decks and offer you that world. But I'll do it because I have no intention of losing you."

"Justin—"

"No, the subject is closed for now. We'll cover it more later, believe me, but there's something else we need to discuss before we get to Maple Tree."

"What?"

"Tonight. The hour we're arriving back in town."

"I told you that I don't care what the gossips say about me."

"Don't you think that's rather selfish of you? What about your father? What you do reflects on him. Do you think it's fair to Vern to have to defend you, or keep silent while people are saying less than flattering things about his daughter? He's a good man, a decent, loving father. He doesn't deserve this hassle, not for a minute."

"Oh," Holly said. "I didn't realize that he . . . You're right. I *have* been terribly selfish and self-centered. My father shouldn't have to pay the price for what I did tonight."

Score one for Justin Hope, he thought smugly. He'd just gotten the ball back in his court. Now all he had to do was play it right. Love was exhausting. But worth it. Oh, yes, Holly Chambers was most definitely worth it.

She pressed her fingertips to her temples. "I've got to think. Don't drive so fast, Justin. I need time to sort this through, figure out how to handle it so that my father doesn't pay the consequences for my actions."

"*We'll* figure it out together. After all, I'm the other half of this scandal, and I'm just as guilty of setting Vern up for potential distress. So, let's calm down and get serious here. We'll put our own problems aside and concentrate on coming up with a plan that will protect Vern."

"How about . . . we ran out of gas?" she suggested, raising her eyebrows.

"How quaint," Justin said dryly. "They won't buy it for a second."

"I didn't think so," she said miserably.

He narrowed his eyes and drummed his fingers on the steering wheel. "Try this one," he said slowly. "Yes, this could work very well."

"I'm listening."

"We need to get the gossip mill off the subject of what time we got back to Maple Tree and back on the sweet-patootie, romantic track. So, we give them a romantic reason why we were out till dawn."

"We do?"

"Absolutely. I'm so brilliant sometimes, I amaze myself."

"Justin, would you just spit it out?"

"Right. The citizens of Maple Tree will be tickled pink as pudding when they hear that we came home late because I was proposing marriage to you, and you were accepting."

"What!"

"This has nothing to do with the fact that I actually did propose to you. You turned me down, of course, but that's beside the point. This plan is separate and apart from what actually happened. Our mission now is to protect your father."

"Justin Hope, I refuse to have the busybodies of Maple Tree believing that I'm going to marry you, because I am *not* going to marry you."

He sighed dramatically. "Poor Vern."

"Oh, good grief, what a mess."

"If you hate my plan, then come up with another one."

"I don't have another one, Justin, and you know it."

He shrugged. "I rest my case."

Holly threw up her hands. "I guess we'll use your idea. We'll tell my father and Melinda that time just got away from us, but we realize no one will believe that."

Justin chuckled. "I don't believe it, either. I was there, remember?"

"Justin, please, I'm trying to think this through. So, okay, we're planning to be married."

If only that were true, he thought.

"Yes," she said, nodding, "I think that announcement will definitely overshadow the one about our coming home at dawn." She paused. "Later, of course, I'll have some explaining to do when you leave and—"

"Don't worry about that now," he interrupted.

"Just how long are you planning on staying in Maple Tree?"

"As long as it takes to convince you that you

and I were meant to have a lifetime together. I thought I made that clear."

She sighed. "Nothing is clear to me at the moment."

"Just concentrate on our plan to protect Vern. That's enough to zero in on for now."

"Okay. Oh, I'm so tired."

"We're almost home, my sweet patootie."

"Justin, shut up with your sweet-patootie garbage. There's no audience here to appreciate it."

"Right."

"Well, I must say," Vern said, "you two are certainly considerate young people. I'm very touched to think you'll go to such lengths to keep the tongue-waggers away from me."

"It's not your fault Justin and I lost track of time," Holly said, fiddling with her coffee mug.

It was late morning, and Holly, Justin, Melinda, and Vern were sitting at the kitchen table.

"No, indeed not," Justin said, smiling pleasantly, "not your fault at all, Vern. I'm going to take a stroll downtown and set the wheels in motion. I estimate that by dinnertime tonight all and everyone will know that Holly Chambers and Justin Hope intend to be married."

That sounded beautiful, Holly thought. Very, very beautiful. If only . . .

"I'm so happy for you, for all of us," Melinda said, then sniffed. "A wedding, a family, a—"

"Melinda," Holly said sternly, "this is a charade, remember?"

"Oh." Melinda looked quickly at Justin, who

winked at her. "Yes, of course it is. I know that. We all know that." She smiled brightly. "Sure."

"Yep," Vern said, nodding, "we know that."

Holly frowned. "Is it my imagination, or are you people acting strangely?"

"I'm not," Vern said. "Are you, Melinda?"

"Me? No, not at all. I'm acting like my perfectly normal self."

"You're just tired, Holly," Justin said, patting her hand. "Why don't you try to catch a nap this afternoon?"

"Yes, I am tired," she said, "but I still think you're all— "

Melinda jumped to her feet. "Time to make up beds, Holly. I'm ready for action." She started toward the door. "Coming?"

"Yes." Holly stood, glanced at Justin and Vern, received bland looks from them in return, and followed Melinda from the room.

Justin rolled his eyes heavenward and let out a pent-up swish of air. "I think I'm too old for all of this."

Vern smiled and shook his head. "Things sure weren't this complicated in my day, I can tell you that. A man came courting, made his intentions known to the lady in question and her father, and it all went fine from there."

"Hey, I'm ready, willing, and able," Justin said. "It's that stubborn daughter of yours who's holding up the show. I sure hope she starts liking the idea of being engaged to me, per se. Everyone is going to be fussing over her, asking her when the wedding is, all that jazz. I, of course, have to stick like glue to my sweet patootie. If all of this gets

Holly to drop her guard a little, she'll be able to see that I intend to make the changes in my life-style as I said I would, and I'll be happy doing it."

"You're fighting very hard for my girl," Vern said seriously.

"And I'll win. I have to, Vern." Justin got to his feet. "That's it, bottom line. I have to. I'm going downtown."

"Good luck," Vern said as Justin left the room.

"I need all the luck I can get," he called over his shoulder.

"Don't give up on her, Justin," Vern said to the empty room. "She loves you and she needs you, son."

"The sun was up before they got back," a woman said.

"So I heard," another woman said in an appropriately shocked voice. "I just never would have dreamed that Holly would do such a thing. And that Justin Hope seemed like such a nice young man too. I never met him, but I saw him, and he's handsome as the day is long. Martha Sue said she would have been proud to call him her grandson, but now . . . tsk, tsk, Vern must just be beside himself about Holly's behavior."

Justin bent over farther, his nose practically pressed to the can of shaving cream on the drugstore shelf.

The old hens sure weren't wasting any time, he thought, shaking his head. They probably had hearts of gold, but give them a juicy bit of gossip and they took off running like fullbacks intent on making it to the goal line.

He grabbed two cans of shaving cream and straightened, remembering at the last moment to flash one of his very best, charm-the-socks-off-'em smiles.

"Good morning, ladies," he said.

"Oh, saints save us," one of the women said, splaying her hand on her chest. She was small and thin, and appeared to be in her late sixties.

The other woman was big-boned and tall, tipping the scale, Justin was convinced, at an easy two hundred pounds. She was seventy-five if she was a day, and had perfected the art of poking her nose in the air and sniffing in righteous indignation, which she proceeded to do.

"I'm Justin Hope," he said, still smiling to beat the band. "And you two lovely ladies are . . . ?" He raised his eyebrows.

"I'm—I'm Florence Fay Falsworth," said the small woman, "and this is Esther Smith."

Esther sniffed again and lifted her nose another notch.

"My pleasure," Justin said, bowing slightly. "May I come around to your side of the aisle? I'm in need of assistance, and I can tell that you're both wise and generous ladies."

"Oh, well, I . . ." Florence Fay said, patting the bun at the back of her skinny neck.

"Thank you ever so much," Justin said.

"Why are you speaking to that rogue?" Esther whispered to Florence Fay.

"Oh, well, I . . ." Florence Fay said.

Still holding the two cans of shaving cream, he strode around the end of the aisle and stopped in front of the pair. Florence Fay, he observed, looked ready to announce that she was about to have an attack of the vapors, although he'd never been sure just what the vapors were. Esther, on the other hand, appeared as though she would gladly tear him limb from limb and enjoy every minute of it. Smile, he told himself. He had to remember to smile.

"I can't tell you how much I appreciate this," he said. "You see, even as much as I love my Holly, I have yet to learn all her little likes and dislikes. Take this shaving cream, for example. Should I get the regular kind or the menthol-minty? I just don't know which Holly would prefer."

Florence Fay leaned closer for a better look at the cans. Esther frowned and didn't budge.

"After all," Justin went on, sliding a glance at the formidable Esther, "when a man is going to marry the only woman he's ever loved, he does want to please her in every way possible."

Florence Fay's eyes widened. "Marry? The only woman he . . . you have ever . . . oh, my stars, how romantic. You and Holly are . . . isn't that just the sweetest thing, Esther?"

Esther simply continued to frown with her nose in the air.

"It was no small task getting Holly to agree to marry me," Justin said. "I had to talk for hours to convince her that we belonged together for all our days. Before I knew it, it was nearly dawn when we were heading back to Maple Tree."

"*That's* why you were out all night?" Florence Fay asked. "You were proposing marriage to Holly?"

"Oh, yes, ma'am. And she finally agreed to become my wife. Losing a night's sleep is a small

price to pay when you consider the final outcome."
He paused. "Goodness, you don't suppose folks
will think poorly of Holly and me because we were
out until dawn, do you? The thought just never
occurred to me because I was so determined to
plead and win my case with the woman of my
heart. Time had no meaning."

"Oh, my dear boy," Florence Fay said, "don't
you give it another thought. If there's any gossip
going around about the hour you came home,
we'll set people straight. I'll personally see to it
that word is spread that you and Holly are to be
married."

She was probably a pro at word-spreading, Justin thought, suppressing a smile. "Thank you,
ma'am."

"Use the regular shaving cream," Esther said
suddenly. "I can't abide a man who smells like a
perfume counter. And tell Holly to wear white at
your wedding. Her marriage to Jimmy Chambers
doesn't count for anything because he was bad to
the core. Holly has every right to be a bride in
white. Come on, Florence Fay, we must go calling
on Martha Sue, Gracie Hill . . . Well, we have a lot
to do to be sure there's no more naughty whispers
about our Holly and Justin."

"Have you set a date for the nuptials?" Florence
Fay asked Justin.

"Not yet. I'll get back to you."

"Excellent," Florence Fay said, beaming. "Oh,
this is so exciting, and sooo . . ."

"Romantic," Justin said. "Yes, I know."

"Good day to you," Florence Fay said, "and our
best wishes to Holly."

"Yes, indeed," Esther said. "Hurry along now, Florence Fay."

The two women bustled down the aisle, and Justin smiled with satisfaction.

Well, he'd done it, he mused as he replaced the shaving cream. Maple Tree would soon be buzzing with the news that Holly Chambers was to marry Justin Hope. Their night together wasn't scandalous, it was romantic, for crying out loud.

Justin shoved his hands into his pants pockets and left the store. If only, he thought, it were all true. If only Holly *had* agreed to marry him. Their lovemaking had been incredible, his desire was still at the boil, but he wanted a commitment from Holly along with her declaration of love and her willingness to make love. He wanted her to be his wife, his partner, his other half. But he hadn't won the whole fight yet. No, not yet.

When Justin entered Holly's Bed and Breakfast, Holly was coming out of the office. He leaned against the counter and smiled at her.

"Hi," he said. "Why the frown?"

"You've been busy. I've had three calls already expressing gushing delight over the news that you and I are to be married."

He laughed. "Gushing delight? Not bad."

She plunked her elbows on the counter and rested her chin in her hands, her frown deepening. "I hate this deception, Justin. I know, don't say it, it's best this way in order to protect my father, but still . . . I feel like a fraud, a total phony-baloney."

"I don't like it, either," Justin said, all traces of his smile gone.

"You don't?"

"No. If I had my way, every word being spoken would be the truth. You would be engaged to me, and we'd be making our plans for a future together."

"Justin, don't. There's no point in saying all that because—"

"Yes, there is a point," he interrupted. He gripped her wrists, pulling her hands free of her chin as he leaned toward her. "I'm going to keep saying it, Holly, over and over, and at the same time I'm going to be proving to you that I mean every word. There will be no reason left for you to doubt me." He moved closer until his lips were nearly touching hers. "Or to doubt yourself for loving me."

He dropped her wrists and wove his fingers through her soft curls. His lips found hers in a searing kiss, and her hands circled his neck as she responded instantly to the eager, hungry demands of his lips and tongue. The counter stood as a solid, unyielding barrier between them, and a groan of frustration rumbled in Justin's chest.

He lifted his head and managed a smile. "Climb up on this counter and I'll ravish your body."

She laughed and dropped her hands from his neck. The highly charged spell was broken, but her cheeks were flushed and desire still shone in her dark eyes.

"Up on the counter?" she repeated. "Even you couldn't produce a reasonable explanation for the gossipers as to why we were . . . well, you couldn't."

"Try me."

"No, thanks," she said, still smiling.

He drew his thumb over her lips. "Ah, Holly, I love you," he said, his voice low and serious. "It felt so right telling those old gals downtown that we're going to be married. Then as I was walking back here I got an ache in my gut because I know you haven't agreed to become my wife. You've still got a wall between us that's as real as this counter."

"Justin . . ."

"Listen, I've got to make some more phone calls, but I'd like you to think about something, all right? I told you that I can set up an office as a sort of central command post anywhere I choose. I'd like to keep the apartment in New York so it's there when we want to use it. We could see plays, go to concerts, enjoy all that wonderful, but crazy city has to offer. It would be our—our fantasy land, where we'd go when we wanted to enjoy the bright lights and excitement for a few days."

He smiled warmly at her. "But our home?" he went on. "The place where we'll raise our children? You can pick the spot. If you want us to live here in Maple Tree, no problem. It's up to you."

"You'd—you'd live in Maple Tree?"

"If that's what you want, what will make you happy, then we'll stay right here. We'll have the best of both of our worlds, don't you see? As for Holly's Bed and Breakfast . . . well, we'll work that out. I'm not crazy about waking up to an empty bed because you're downstairs fixing breakfast at dawn for a bunch of fishermen, but we can compromise on that too. There's nothing standing in our way, Holly. Nothing . . . except you and your fears." He kissed her quickly. "Think about it. I've got to get some files from my room, then I'm going to hole up in the office again."

Holly watched as he bounded up the stairs two at a time. Her mind raced as she replayed his words in her mind. The best of both of their worlds? Was it possible? She loved Justin so much, and he was trying hard to make her realize they did have a future together if she'd only give them the chance. Justin Hope living in Maple Tree? Holly Chambers flitting around New York City? No, it was absurd. Or was it?

"Holly!" Melinda came running down the hall, her face pale and her eyes frantic. "Holly! Justin! Holly!"

"Melinda, what is it?" Holly asked, hurrying around the counter.

"Your father," Melinda said, gasping for breath. "He was on the ladder trimming trees and . . . oh, God, Holly, he fell and he said he thinks his leg is broken, and"—tears filled her eyes—"and he needs help, and . . ."

"What's wrong?" Justin asked, racing back down the stairs.

"My father . . ." Holly started. "Justin, call an ambulance. Please. Call." She ran toward the back of the house.

The hospital in Maple Tree was small but well-equipped, and had an expertly trained staff. Vern Richards was whisked away behind green doors that had a sign that read AUTHORIZED PERSONNEL ONLY.

Holly stood outside the doors, staring at them and wringing her hands. She was vaguely aware that Justin had come to her side and circled her shoulders with his arm.

"Holly," he said gently, "come sit down. Vern is going to be fine. He never lost consciousness, and if the language he was muttering is any indication, he's mad as hell, which is a good sign."

"I hate to see him in pain," she said, her voice trembling. "It's not fair that this should have happened to him."

Justin kissed her on the temple. "Don't set me up to say some corny cliché like Life isn't always fair. We'll sit right over here where we can watch the doors. Melinda is calling Mrs. Hill and asking her to go to your place in case any of the guests need something."

Holly nodded and allowed Justin to lead her across the room to a sofa.

"You're white as a ghost," he said, sitting down next to her. "Vern looked better than you do. Try to relax a little."

Tears filled her eyes. "When I got to him where he was lying in the yard, he said, 'Well, I've done it up good this time, my girl.' Oh, Justin, I don't want him to be hurt."

"Because you love him. We never want those we love to be hurt, but sometimes it happens, and we can't do anything but be there for that person to give them whatever they need. I was far too slow in realizing that in regard to Melinda, but I understand it now. Vern knows you're here for him, Holly."

She looked up at him. "You're a wonderful man, Justin Hope."

"I'm a man in love, Holly Chambers."

Their eyes held for a long moment, then Holly sighed and redirected her attention to the green doors.

Melinda came around the corner. "Mrs. Hill is going right over to the house. What did the doctor say?"

"Nothing yet," Justin said. "They'll have to take X rays and the whole routine."

Melinda slouched into a chair. "I was so scared when he fell. I just—" She shook her head as tears choked off her words.

"You did fine," Holly said. "You came for help just as you should have. We're fortunate you were in the yard with him." She looked at the doors again. "I hope Doc Jenkins is here. He and my dad are close friends, have been for many years. Doc Jenkins is the one my father would want tending to him."

"How long do we have to wait before they tell us something?" Melinda asked.

"I'm not sure," Justin said.

It seemed like an eternity.

Holly alternated between staring at the green doors, the clock, getting up and pacing, then sitting back down close to Justin.

No one spoke. No one knew what to say.

A little over an hour after they'd arrived, the green doors opened and a short, gray-haired man came out. Holly, Justin, and Melinda were instantly on their feet.

"Oh, Doc Jenkins," Holly said, "I'm so glad you were here to help my father. How is he?"

Lines crinkled by the doctor's eyes as he smiled. "Ornery as all get-out. Vern Richards is not a happy man."

"But how is he?" Holly asked.

"He's going to be fine," Doc Jenkins said. "He has a clean break of his right leg below the knee. He'll have a heavy cast on it for a while, then I'll change it to a walking cast. He was lucky really. I told him he had no business up on a ladder trimming trees. The amazing part is he agreed with me, said it was time he slowed down and did what he's been dreaming of doing."

Holly frowned. "What do you mean? What has he been dreaming of doing?"

"Vern's been talking about it for a couple of years now during our poker games," Doc Jenkins said. "He wants to move into that cabin he has over by Natchez Lake. He's going to fish to his heart's content, read, putter around. Yep, sounds good to me. I'm glad he's finally going to do it."

"I never knew he wanted that," Holly said. "He hasn't said one word to me about this."

"Maybe I'm talking out of turn then," Doc Jenkins said, stroking his chin. "Vern probably wanted to tell you himself. Well, I'll apologize to him for that. It's all working out fine, anyway. Vern didn't feel he could leave you alone to run the bed and breakfast, so he kept quiet. Scuttlebutt around the hospital is that you're getting married, Holly, so Vern is free to move on over to his cabin. Took breaking his leg to make him see he was overdue to go after that dream of his. Life is crazy sometimes, the way it works."

"Yes," Holly whispered, "it certainly is."

"Now then," the doctor said, "you go on home and come back tonight to see Vern. I gave him a shot that will have him sleeping like a baby for hours. He'll be awake and complaining by suppertime."

"Thank you," Holly said absently. "Thank you very much."

"Don't you worry about Vern. I'll have him fit as a fiddle in no time so I can go visit him at that cabin and do some serious fishing. That sure does sound fine. See you folks later." He turned and went down the hall.

"Let's go, Holly," Justin said. "I think you could use a nap too."

She looked up at him, a stricken expression on her face. "I never knew about his dream, Justin. My father didn't tell me he wanted something other than the bed and breakfast."

"Holly . . ."

"He stayed because of me, because I was clinging to that house like a lifeline, and I couldn't run the bed and breakfast alone. But now he says he's going to the cabin. Doc Jenkins thinks I'm getting married, but my father knows I'm not. I guess . . . I guess he's going to move to the cabin, anyway. Well, that's fine. I mean, I'm a grown woman who's perfectly capable of running a bed and breakfast on her own. But why didn't my dad tell me about his dream?"

"Holly," Justin said, "it's not exactly the way you think it is. Vern wouldn't just up and leave you. The truth of the matter is, Vern knows I love you, that I want to marry you. So does Melinda. They helped me convince you to go along with the charade of our being engaged so I could stay close to you."

"My brother is dead meat," Melinda said under her breath.

Holly narrowed her eyes. "This whole business about protecting my father because we stayed out all night was a sham?" She waved a hand in the air. "You all put your heads together and came up with this plan to manipulate me?"

"No, no," Justin said quickly. "Vern and Melinda were simply supporting my fight to win you, to persuade you to marry me. They've been in on it since the sweet-patootie number."

"Dead, dead meat," Melinda said, shaking her head.

"Because they love you," Justin rushed on, "and they know that your marrying me is the best thing for you . . . us . . . and . . . Holly, your face is turning red."

"How dare you all decide what I should do with my life," Holly said, her eyes flashing with anger. "Justin Hope, don't you ever speak to me again. Don't touch me or look at me. Ever. Melinda, I'll excuse you because of your age. But when Vern Richards is back on his feet, I'm going to break his other leg."

Justin raised his hands in a gesture of peace. "Holly, please, you're taking this all wrong. Calm down. I love you, remember? And you love me."

"You manipulated me," she said, planting her fists on her hips. "You even went so far as to enlist the help of my father and your young sister. You're used to winning, aren't you, Justin, in your megabucks, big-business world? That's not how love works. You tried to make me dance to your tune, like a marionette with you pulling the strings. Well, guess what? You lose. You can take a flying leap, Justin Hope, because I never want to see you again."

She pushed past him and ran down the hall and out the hospital.

Justin blinked, then shook his head. "Dammit," he muttered, "what happened? All I was trying to do was get across to her that we all love her."

"It sounded terrible, Justin," Melinda said, "like Mr. Richards was putting a child in your care, knowing she'd be looked after and freeing him to pursue his dream. Holly needs to be loved as a woman, on a one-to-one basis, by the man she loves. She probably feels like a kid with a squad of baby-sitters. In short, brother dear, you blew it."

"Well, hell," Justin said, starting toward the door. Melinda hurried to keep up with him. "I'm running out of patience, Melinda." He pushed open the door with more force than was necessary. "I've knocked myself out trying to prove to Holly how much I love her. It's time she lightened up, started trusting and believing in me. She says she loves me, but I keep taking it in the chops. I've had it, really had it." He strode toward his car with long, heavy strides.

"Uh-oh," Melinda said, running after him. "War has been declared in Maple Tree, Wisconsin."

Nine

Holly didn't walk the mile and a half from the hospital back to the house . . . she stomped. She looked, she realized, about six years old, which was when she'd perfected the art of stomping to her room whenever she was sent there for being sassy. But she didn't care, so she stomped, tears streaming down her cheeks. She swiped them away and ignored everyone who waved or called to her.

She'd never been so angry or hurt or confused in her entire life.

She was the victim of a conspiracy, she told herself.

She was deeply loved by a man who had left no stone unturned to win her love in return.

Her own father was in on the loathsome plot.

A father who wanted to see his daughter happy at long last.

She had been treated like a brainless child instead of the mature woman she was.

She was held in the iron fist of childish fears that were keeping her from moving forward as a woman should.

She never wanted to see Justin again.

Oh, God, what if she never saw Justin again? Was never touched, held, kissed, made love to by Justin again? She couldn't bear the thought.

"I'm going out of my mind," she said.

Inside Holly's Bed and Breakfast she quickly told Mrs. Hill that Vern was going to be fine, although he had, indeed, broken his leg. Mrs. Hill took one look at Holly's tearstained face and insisted that she go rest.

"I'm doing just fine here, dear," Mrs. Hill said. "The phone is ringing off the hook with those wishing to congratulate you and Justin on your engagement, and others just learning about Vern's accident. I adore answering the phone. Oh, Justin had a call from Paris. I took down the message very carefully, don't you fear. Imagine getting a telephone call from Paris, France. Will Justin be along soon so I can tell him he's been asked to call this man in Paris right away?"

"I guess Justin and Melinda will be here any minute," Holly said, glancing at the front door. She couldn't see Justin, not now. She was such a confused, befuddled mess, there was no telling what she might say or do. And she certainly didn't need Mrs. Hill as a witness to whatever it might be. "If you're sure you don't mind, I think I'll go lie down."

"You go right ahead," Mrs. Hill said, flapping a hand at her. "If the truth be known, Holly, you look simply awful."

"Oh, thanks," Holly muttered, starting toward the stairs. "That really perks me up."

In her room she pulled off her shoes, then flung herself across the bed. Once again she saw in her mind's eye her father as he lay in pain on the ground beneath the tree, and her tears started to flow.

"Oh, Daddy," she whispered, burying her face in her pillow, "I don't want you to be hurt. And, darn you, Dad, for teaming up with Justin against me."

Against her, or for her, she wondered in the next instant. Oh, she couldn't think anymore. She was so tired, physically and emotionally drained. Later she'd sort through the jumble in her mind, one unanswered question at a time. Later, after she had had a short nap. Just . . . a . . . snooze.

With the tears still wet on her cheeks, and hugging her pillow as though it were a comforting teddy bear, Holly slept.

Justin sank back in the desk chair in Holly's office and squeezed the bridge of his nose. The receiver to the telephone was pressed to his ear, and he nodded as the man on the other end continued to speak.

"That's about where we stand, Justin," the man said finally. "The investors have flown in from all over the world, ready to sign on the dotted line. This is one of the biggest deals you've ever put together, and they've been waiting for months to get the word that you're prepared to set it in motion."

"So what's their problem, Philip? Everyone received preview copies of the contracts and had their lawyers go over them. All they have to do now is sign the actual contracts, turn over their checks, and break out the champagne."

"They don't trust me yet, Justin. They know you and are used to dealing with you. This change in command came very quickly, and in the middle of a multimillion-dollar deal. They're nervous, and they're wondering why you're not here. They're not going to play ball unless they see your gorgeous baby blues when they sign those contracts. Actually, I don't blame them. They're protecting themselves against an unknown. I respect that."

"So do I, except this is a lousy time for me to be jetting off to Paris," Justin said. He looked up at the ceiling, picturing Holly in her room, wondering what was going through her mind. He sighed. "Okay. I gotta do what I gotta do. Tell the investors I'll be there as quickly as possible, and I'm picking up the tab for their extra days in Paris. You plan to be with me every minute once I arrive, Philip. You'll present the actual contracts, and I'll be in the background. They can witness the change of command, for Pete's sake."

"Got it. See you soon, Justin."

"All right, Philip," Justin said wearily.

He slowly replaced the receiver and reached for the telephone book. Then he rested his hand on the book and stared up at the ceiling again.

Dammit, he fumed, he didn't want to go to Paris now. Everything was falling apart with Holly. But he'd meant what he'd said to Melinda. He'd really had it with beating his head against a wall, trying to convince Holly to trust and believe in him, in his love for her. Yes, he knew she had deep scars from her experience with Jimmy Chambers, but Justin was tired of fighting ghosts.

He shook his head and flipped open the telephone book. Maybe, he mused, it was just as well he was going to Paris. His patience was down to zip, his anger very close to the surface. That final scene in the hospital with Holly had capped it. He needed to get away and recharge his mental batteries. If he tried to talk to Holly now, he'd be torn between wanting to make love to her for hours and the urge to wring her pretty neck for being so damn stubborn about admitting they could have a wonderful future together.

He stared across the room. But was it dangerous to leave Holly alone to think and stew, he pondered. Given time and space, what direction would her thoughts take her? Would she miss him or dismiss him? Well, he had no choice but to go to Paris. The deal was the result of many months of tedious work, and would ultimately provide jobs for a great many people. If it fell through now, the ramifications would be far-reaching.

But what would he find when he returned to Maple Tree? Would Holly welcome him back with open arms and a warm, loving smile? Or would she decide during his absence that she could survive very nicely without him, thank you very much. Would he be reduced to only memories and be sent packing? Lord, what a depressing, totally unacceptable thought. They were in love with each other, dammit.

"Quit thinking," he muttered. "You're driving yourself bonkers."

Holly stirred and opened her eyes. A golden glow filled the room, indicating the spring sunset was in full splendor and darkness would soon fall.

She'd had a long nap, she realized. Without much effort she was sure she could close her eyes and not surface again until morning. To sleep was to avoid thinking, and she was not yet prepared to tackle the scrambled entity she was loosely referring to as her brain. So, she'd go back to sleep and—

"Dad," she said suddenly.

She bolted off the bed, grabbed clean clothes, and headed down the hall to the shower. A short time later she was back in her room and pulling on a pale green lightweight sweater and off-white linen slacks. After a dab of lip gloss and a flick of the brush through her curls, she sank onto the bed.

Well, she thought dismally, she certainly seemed to spend a lot of time sitting on the edges of beds thinking these days. At least she wasn't hugging the pillow again like a child.

She stiffened. A child. That was exactly how she'd been behaving when she'd flung those hateful words at Justin, telling him she never wanted to see him again.

And her childish attitude went even further than the incident at the hospital. She'd been clinging to the safety of her painful past rather than taking a chance on an unknown future. She'd clung to the house and town of her youth, and fought against all and everyone who would take any of it away from her. Fought against Justin, the man she loved.

It was suddenly all so clear, she realized, like sunshine bursting through a cloudy sky to bring the warmth of spring to her chilled soul. She was awakening as the woman she was meant to be. The woman who was deeply and forever in love with Justin.

"Oh, Justin," she whispered. "I'm so sorry."

She rushed from the room and was halfway down the stairs when Justin came in the front door. She stopped, her hand on the banister, and met his gaze as he closed the door and looked up at her. Melinda was behind the counter, Holly noticed absently, instead of Mrs. Hill.

Holly's heartbeat speeded up and desire throbbed deep within her at the mere sight of Justin. Oh, how she loved him.

"Justin—"

"I just came from the hospital," he said brusquely. "I wanted to see Vern before I left. I was hoping you'd be awake by the time I got back."

Melinda inched her way from behind the counter. "I think I'll have some dinner. 'Bye." She hurried down the hall.

Holly forced her trembling legs to move down the remaining stairs. The entranceway separated her from Justin as she looked at him intently.

"Left?" she repeated, finding it difficult to breathe. "You're—you're leaving Maple Tree?"

"I have an important deal to handle in Paris. It's something that only I can take care of this time. I hope it's all right if Melinda stays here while I'm gone."

"Of course it's all right." Holly shook her head. "You're flying to Paris? Now? I mean, you returned the phone call from there, and you're suddenly winging your way to Paris?"

Justin crossed his arms and stared up at the ceiling. "Here it comes, right on cue." He looked at her again, a muscle jumping along his jaw. "You're going to pick up this trip to Paris and use it like a sledgehammer on me, beat me to death with the evidence that our worlds are too different for us to ever have a future together."

"No, Justin."

"I've tried, Holly," he went on, not listening to her. "God knows I've tried to fight your ghosts and fears, to prove to you that you didn't choose the wrong man to love this time, because I love you every bit as much in return. I've done everything I could possibly think of to win this fight, to win you, even to the point of asking the help of those around you who love you. For what purpose? Answer me that, Holly."

"Justin . . ."

He rushed on. "Every time I made an inch of progress, you pulled us back a yard. You refused to believe in me, trust me, give me any time or faith. I was sincerely trying to show you that I've changed my values and priorities. Yes, I have to go to Paris, to take charge of a situation that I'd passed on to someone else too soon so I could be with you."

"Justin . . ."

"I can't do it anymore," he said, nearly yelling.

"I'm tired, understand? Tired of pleading my case, walking on eggs around you for fear I'll do or say something that will set you off. Melinda said you probably feel as though I treated you like a child. Well, if the shoe fits, lady, wear it, because I'm seeing childish tantrums, and you're using childish excuses of past mistakes as an escape from the reality of today. Today, Holly, includes loving me as a woman, my partner, my equal. You're hanging on to the past, as painful as it was, because it's familiar, you know exactly what it is. Go ahead and hide behind your wall. I don't have the energy left to try to tear it down. I love you but, dammit, I've had enough."

He picked up the suitcase, he'd left behind the counter, then walked with heavy steps back to the door. Holly hurried to his side, placing one hand on his arm.

"Justin, wait, please, don't go, not like this."

He looked down at her, and Holly saw the wave of pain that crossed his features, then settled in the depths of his blue eyes. His voice was low and hoarse when he spoke again.

"Wait for what? To hear another long list of why we can't make it together? No thanks. Maybe I was the one who fantasized this time. Fantasized that you loved me as much as I do you. Did you even try to meet me halfway? I don't think so. I was supposed to run the whole distance, then allow you to pass judgment on everything I offered you. Well, the race is over." He laughed, a sharp, bitter sound. "I lost." He opened the door. "I'll be back as soon as I can to get Melinda. Good-bye, Holly." He looked at her for a long moment.

Before she could say anything else, Justin was gone, closing the door behind him with a decisive click. She stood statue-still, and a minute later heard his car start. The sound of the rumbly engine faded as he drove away from the house.

On legs that threatened to give way beneath her, Holly left the house, deciding to walk to the hospital. She needed the time to compose herself before she saw her father. She walked slowly, her mind racing.

Every word Justin had spoken had been true, she knew that, but she'd gathered her courage and faced those truths too late. On one issue, though, he was wrong. When he'd said he was flying to Paris, she hadn't been ready to use his trip as evidence of their incompatible life-styles. She had finally realized just how important and powerful Justin really was. She had been going to wish him every success in his dealings in Paris, and assure him she'd be waiting for him when he returned.

Holly sighed. She'd never had a chance to say those words. Justin had assumed, and with just cause, that her reaction to his leaving for Paris would be as childish as her previous performances. Oh, how clearly she could see things now, and they didn't cast her in a favorable light. But the child had, at long last, emerged as the woman.

A woman in love.

Yet it was too late. Justin was gone.

"But he'll be back," she said aloud, quickening her step. Unless he simply sent Melinda a plane ticket to fly to New York, Justin would be back to get his sister. She had one more chance to prove to Justin Hope that she was free of her past, had crumbled her wall into dust and was prepared to stand by his side for the remainder of their days. She was the one fighting for their love now and, oh, dear God, she just had to win.

When Holly entered her father's hospital room, he was propped up against the pillows, the blankets tented above his injured leg.

She managed a small smile, but her voice trembled when she spoke. "Well, I've done it up good this time, Dad."

"Yep," he said, and held out his arms to her. "Come here, my girl."

"How's your leg?"

"Broken. Come here."

She went into her father's embrace, savoring his hug as she'd done countless times as she'd grown up. But this time, she knew, a hug wasn't going to make it better. She straightened, unable to stop two tears that slid down her cheeks.

"He's gone, Dad." She swept the tears away. "Justin is gone. Angry, hurt, not even sure I love him."

"He'll be back. Melinda is here."

"I know. I have one more chance. I was hanging on to all the wrong things, wasn't I?"

Vern nodded.

"I've let go of the past, Dad. I want a future with Justin. I love him so much, and I need him. Maybe it's too late to win him now, but I'm going to try with all that I am."

"That's my girl," Vern said. "Justin truly loves

you, Holly. He was in rough shape when he came by here. He feels defeated, beaten by ghosts he couldn't even see."

"I know. I've made so many mistakes, and the frightening part is, I'm not certain how to start undoing the damage I've done. I don't know how to convince Justin that I've changed. I wouldn't believe and trust in him when he was saying that to me."

"Listen to your heart, Holly. That's what I did when I made the decision to move to the cabin. It's time for me to go. It's time for you to live and love again."

She leaned over and kissed him on the cheek. "I love you, Dad."

"Be happy, Holly. You're long overdue to be happy." He smiled. "Now, how about some fussing about my poor broken leg? Seems to me that if I have to carry this ton of concrete around, I deserve some sympathy."

She matched his smile. "One serving of sympathy coming right up."

"There you go, Philip," Justin said, handing him some papers. "You are now officially in charge of the Paris office of Hope Enterprises."

"I still can't believe it," Philip said. "I question your sanity, but I'm sure not complaining."

"I'm going to sell off some of my other holdings," Justin said, "cut back and slow down."

"Changing your life-style, huh?"

"Yes, it's due. I want to spend more time with

my sister. Delegating authority has helped some, but I still have my fingers in too many pies."

"Your sister? I would have said by the changes you're making in your life that you had a very special lady waiting for you back home. You've been here over three weeks getting the details squared away. I figured you were in for one wing-dinger of a welcome when you got back."

Justin stared out of the office window. "No, not the kind of welcome you're referring to. My sixteen-year-old sister is the only . . . the only one waiting for me. Only Melinda."

Just after noon two days later, memories of Holly slammed against Justin's heart and mind as Maple Tree came into view in the distance. He drove slowly, savoring his memories of his time spent with Holly. It was a luxury, he knew, this remembering, that he hadn't allowed himself to indulge in while he was in Paris. Each time Holly's image had flitted before his mind's eye, he'd pushed it firmly away, only to have to repeat the process soon after. She had followed him through his days and crept into his dreams at night, causing him to toss and turn, aching for her, missing her.

He drove past the sign welcoming him to Maple Tree, Wisconsin. This was where he'd found Holly, fallen in love with her, then lost her before she'd ever truly been his. Had he given up his fight for her too soon? No, there had been nothing more he could do. He'd lost. And it hurt. The future stretched before him like a barren wasteland, devoid of color and warmth. It was simply empty, like the hollow feeling in his soul.

Justin sighed. He had wired Melinda, telling her of his arrival time in Maple Tree and instructing her to be packed and ready to go. He was assuming she would tell Holly and Holly would make herself scarce, not wishing to see him. A coward's way out? Definitely. But just being in Maple Tree was ripping him up. He would rush in, snatch up his sister, and get the hell out of there. Ah, damn it, Holly.

Suddenly Justin was pulled from his tormented thoughts by a strange sense of déjà vu. His eyes darted quickly back and forth as he drove down the main street of town. The spring day was warm, the sky a bright blue dotted with fluffy marshmallow clouds, and cars were parked in front of the shops.

But there were no people on the sidewalks of Maple Tree, Wisconsin!

Justin groaned. Not again, he thought. Another disaster drill? How many memories could his shattering heart take? But wait a minute. He was sure Charlie Potts had said he'd met the state requirement of having four drills. So, why were they having another one? Unless . . . they weren't.

His grip on the steering wheel tightened. Was something *really* wrong this time? Where was everyone? Even the fat dog he'd seen on that first day wasn't around. Good Lord, what was going on here?

Calm down, he told himself. Maybe Charlie Potts was having another drill to show off for Clara Mary. How was *that* romance progressing? Hell, he didn't care. Yes, dammit, he did. He cared about this town and the people in it. He cared about the gossipy busybodies with hearts of gold, who made a stranger feel like a part of a large, warm family. He cared about Vern, who was going after his dream at long last. And he was in love with, would always love, Holly Chambers.

He decided to check out the field where the other drill had been held. If that was what was going on, he'd pass by and go directly to Holly's Bed and Breakfast with the hope that Melinda was waiting for him there. He'd be in and out of Maple Tree before Holly ever knew he'd been there. He wouldn't see her, kiss her, hold or touch her. Ever again.

"Dammit," he muttered. "Well, you'd better let Holly be wounded instead of dead this time, Potts, or she'll have your hide."

As Justin turned the last corner, he frowned. Cars lined the street next to the field and a multitude of people were gathered in the middle of it, but there were no ambulances, fire trucks, or police cars. The crowd was simply standing there. No one was running, no bodies were scattered on the ground. And chairs were assembled in neat rows. Chairs? There was an archway of some sort covered in bright spring flowers. This was not an emergency disaster drill.

Go to Holly's Bed and Breakfast, Justin instructed himself firmly.

He parked the car, turned off the ignition, and got out.

They were having a concert or something, he

thought. Everything was fine, so he should go get Melinda.

His feet seemed to move of their own volition, carrying him through the opening in the fence and across the grass. As he approached, he heard a murmur rise from the crowd, then they parted like a sea of humanity.

And he saw her.

Holly.

He stumbled slightly, then stopped, his heart thundering as he drank in the sight of her. She was wearing an old-fashioned wedding gown of white lace and satin and was holding a bouquet of pink rosebuds. Looking as though she'd stepped out of another era, she was the most beautiful woman, the most exquisite bride he'd ever seen.

Bride?

His Holly was marrying someone other than him?

The hell she was!

He strode forward, vaguely aware that people were smiling at him and a few were patting him on the back. His eyes met Holly's as he walked toward her, and she held his gaze steadily. He stopped in front of her and drew a deep breath, hoping to rein in his raging temper before attempting to speak.

But Holly spoke first.

"Hello, Justin," she said softly with just a trace of a weak smile. "I'm so glad to see you my—my sweet patootie."

He blinked, opened his mouth, then snapped it shut. Sweet patootie? What was Holly up to? What in the hell was going on?

He folded his arms over his chest and continued to look directly into her eyes. "It's good to see you, too, my little corn muffin. Nice outfit."

She took a deep breath, then lifted her chin. "Justin, our secret is out."

"It is?" This ought to be good, he thought. Lord, she was beautiful. He wanted to haul her into his arms and— "Perhaps you'd care to explain?"

"Oh, you bet," she said, nodding.

"Now."

"Well! You see, Justin, everyone now knows that I didn't go to Madison last week for three days to shop. Nope, I didn't do that. They know that you were there, and we had our blood tests, waited the necessary length of time, got our marriage license, and were married by the justice of the peace."

"Everyone knows that, do they?" he said.

He heard a familiar chuckle and turned to see Vern, leaning on crutches and grinning at him. Melinda was next to him, and she waggled her fingers at Justin, a bright smile on her face. Justin glared at both of them, then looked back at Holly.

"Go on with your story, Holly," he said, no hint of a smile on his face. "We were married and . . .?"

Holly swallowed heavily. "I explained to everyone that it was necessary to do it that way, Justin, because you're a very busy man who is needed in all parts of the world to properly conduct your businesses. I told everyone how hard you had worked to become a success, and that as your wife I understood the necessity of your traveling a great deal. I said I would travel with you until we started our family, then stay home with Melinda and our children and wait for you to return to us."

A strange warmth began to curl around Justin's heart and spread throughout him.

"That is why," Holly went on, "I contacted the people who had reservations at Holly's Bed and Breakfast and told them I was booking them in another bed and breakfast in Maple Tree. Holly's Bed and Breakfast is no longer in business, and the house is up for sale, because I'll be leaving here, going with you. You know how folks here love a romantic ending to a story, Justin, and they are so happy for us. It's as though we gave them a gift in return for their caring."

The warmth within Justin filled him, chasing away the chilling ache of loneliness and heartbreak. Dear Lord, how he loved this woman. But . . . just how much of what Holly was saying was true, and what was a portion of her parting gift to these people? Yes, he believed she was leaving Maple Tree, as she couldn't fake placing her guests in other establishments. But was she leaving alone, or with him? Had she recited the role she would have as his wife from her heart, or was it just more of the romantic charade?

"Justin," she said, "the people here have asked us to repeat our vows so that they can feel as though they were really a part of our starting our lives together. What we'll do here today isn't legal or binding, of course."

"I see." The warmth began to ebb as the chill crept slowly back.

"But, Justin?" Holly said, tears filling her eyes

as her voice trembled. "Whether we have two wedding ceremonies, or twenty, or—or none, I want you to know that I love you with all my heart. You're not my sweet patootie, you're my life, my husband, my other half. I'll be your equal partner, your wife, the mother of your children. I am a woman . . . yours. I'll travel with you, be with you, and when our babies are born, I'll wait at home for you. I'm all grown-up now, Justin, so I can't be your sweet patootie anymore, because I have very real, very important duties to perform until death parts us." Tears spilled onto her cheeks. "Do you understand? Do you, Justin?"

The warmth consumed him. The chill was swept into oblivion forever.

Holly had meant every word. She loved him, was ready and willing to take her place at his side as his wife. She was accepting him, believing he wanted and needed his old life-style, not knowing he wanted and needed only her. He'd won. They'd won. The ghosts were beaten. The future was theirs.

"Justin?" she whispered.

"You are," he said, his voice choked with emotion, "my wife, my life. I love you so much."

He reached out and pulled her to him, burying his face in her fragrant curls as he struggled to bring his emotions under control. Then he tipped her head back and kissed her, sealing the commitment they had just made. A collective sigh went up from the crowd.

"It worked. It did," Melinda said. "Ohhh, how romantic."

"Yep," Vern said, smiling.

"I'm just tickled pink as pudding," Mrs. Hill said, dabbing at her eyes with a lace-edged hankie.

"He's like a grandson to me," Martha Sue said smugly. "Just like a grandson."

Justin lifted his head to see desire and love shining in Holly's eyes.

"Will you marry me?" he asked softly.

"A hundred times," she whispered.

And there, surrounded by people who loved them, with the spring sun pouring over them like a waterfall, Holly and Justin made their vows. On their honeymoon, they knew, they would get a marriage license and go through the ceremony again. But to them, this was their wedding day, their forever day, that held the promises of all their tomorrows.

"You may kiss the bride," the minister said.

"A hundred times," Justin said.

"My goodness," Holly said, smiling, "then you'd better get started."

And he did.

Epilogue

The office door burst open and Holly stomped in, her eyes narrowed in fury.

Justin laughed. "Don't tell me. Charlie Potts gave you a dead card again this year."

"Yes, he did, that rat. He said that since I was pregnant he didn't think I should be toted around, dumped in an ambulance, and whisked away, that I was much better off being dead. Even your secretary was wounded. She said she never had that much fun when she worked for you in New York. Clara Mary Potts was wounded, of course. Do you think it's fair for a man to give his wife special treatment?"

Justin walked around the desk and pulled Holly into his embrace. "*I* give *my* wife special treatment."

"That's deliciously different from what I'm talking about."

His hands roamed over her back, then slipped forward to her full breasts and down to the slope of her stomach that held the miracle that was their baby.

"You sure don't feel dead," he said.

"No, actually, I'm feeling more alive by the minute," she said, smiling at him. "Oh, Justin, I'm so happy. Thank you for wanting to live in Maple Tree, and for insisting that we raise our family in this house where I grew up. These walls will ring with laughter. I love you so very much, Mr. Hope."

"I love you too, Mrs. Hope. Where's Melinda?"

"She went fishing with my father."

"Now, that news just tickles me pink as pudding."

His arm around her shoulders, he led her from the room and up the stairs. In the big bed where their child had been conceived, they made sweet, slow, sensuous love through the remaining hours of the afternoon.

And declared their love in whispered endearments.

A hundred times . . .

THE EDITOR'S CORNER

Next month we kick off one of LOVESWEPT's most sizzling summers! First, we bring you just what you've been asking for—

LOVESWEPT GOLDEN CLASSICS

•

We are ushering in this exciting program with four of the titles you've most requested by four of your most beloved authors . . .

•

Iris Johansen's
THE TRUSTWORTHY REDHEAD
(Originally published as LOVESWEPT #35)

•

Billie Green's
TEMPORARY ANGEL
(Originally published as LOVESWEPT #38)

•

Fayrene Preston's
THAT OLD FEELING
(Originally published as LOVESWEPT #45)

•

Kay Hooper's
SOMETHING DIFFERENT
(Originally published as LOVESWEPT #46)

•

With stunning covers—richly colored, beautifully enhanced by the golden signatures of the authors—LOVESWEPT'S GOLDEN CLASSICS are pure pleasure for those of you who missed them five years ago and exquisite "keepers" for the libraries of those who read and loved them when they were first published. Make sure your bookseller holds a set just for you or order the CLASSICS through our LOVESWEPT mail order subscription service.

And now a peek at our six new sensational romances for next month.

We start off with the phenomenal Sandra Brown's TEMPER-ATURES RISING, LOVESWEPT #336. Handsome Scout Ritland is celebrating the opening of a hotel he helped build on a lush South Pacific island when he's lured into a garden by an extraordinarily beautiful woman. But Chantal duPont has more in
(continued)

mind than a romantic interlude on this sultry moonlit night. She wants Scout all right—but to build a bridge, a bridge to connect the island on which she grew up with the mainland. Then there's an accident that Chantal never intended and that keeps Scout her bedridden patient. In the shadow of an active volcano the two discover their fierce hunger for each other . . . and the smoldering passion between them soon explodes with far-reaching consequences. This is Sandra Brown at her best in a love story to cherish. And remember—this wonderful romance is also available in a Doubleday hardcover edition.

Since bursting onto the romance scene with her enormously popular **ALL'S FAIR** (remember the Kissing Bandit?), Linda Cajio has delighted readers with her clever and sensual stories. Here comes an especially enchanting one, **DESPERATE MEASURES,** LOVESWEPT #337. Ellen Kitteridge is an elegant beauty who draws Joe Carlini to her as iron draws a magnet. Wild, virile, Joe pursues her relentlessly. Ellen is terrified because of her early loveless marriage to a treacherous fortune hunter. She runs from Joe, hides from him . . . but she can't escape. And Joe is determined to convince her that her shattered past has nothing to do with their thrilling future together. Linda's **DESPERATE MEASURES** will leave you breathless!

That brilliant new star of romance writing Deborah Smith gives you another thrilling story in *The Cherokee Trilogy,* **TEMPTING THE WOLF,** LOVESWEPT #338. This is the unforgettable tale of a brilliant, maverick Cherokee who was a pro football player and is now a businessman. Of most concern to Erica Gallatin, however, is his total (and threatening) masculinity. James is dangerous, perfection molded in bronze, absolutely irresistible—and he doesn't trust beautiful "non-Indian" women one bit! Erica is determined to get in touch with her heritage as she explores the mystery of Dove's legacy . . . and she's even more determined to subdue her mad attraction to the fierce warrior who is stealing her soul. This is a romance as heartwarming as it is heart-stopping in its intensity.

Judy Gill produces some of the most sensitive love stories we publish. In LOVESWEPT #339, **A SCENT OF ROSES,** she will once again capture your emotions with the exquisite romance of a memorable hero and heroine. Greg Miller is a race car driver who's lost his memory in an accident. His wife, Susan, puts past hurts aside when she agrees to help him recover. At his family's home in the San Juan Islands—a setting made for love—they rediscover the passion they shared . . . but can they
(continued)

compromise on the future? A thrilling story of deep passion and deep commitment nearly destroyed by misunderstanding.

It's always our greatest pleasure to discover and present a brand-new talent. Please give a warm, warm welcome to Courtney Henke, debuting next month with **CHAMELEON, LOVESWEPT #340.** This is a humorous yet emotionally touching romance we suspect you will never forget . . . in large measure because of its remarkable hero. Emma Machlen is a woman with a single purpose when she invades Maxwell Morgan's domain. She's going to convince the cosmetics mogul to buy the unique fragrance her family has developed. She's utterly desperate to make the sale. But she never counts on the surprises Max will have for her, not the least of which is his incredible attractiveness. Enchanted by Emma, drawn to her against his will, Max is turned upside down by this little lady whom he *must* resist. Emma has her work cut out for her in winning over Max . . . but the poor man never has a chance! An absolutely wonderful story!

And what could make for more sizzling reading than another of Helen Mittermeyer's Men of Fire? Nothing I can think of. All the passion, intensity, emotional complexity, richness, and humor you expect in one of Helen's love stories is here in **WHITE HEAT, LOVESWEPT #341.** When Pacer Dillon—that irresistible heartbreaker Helen introduced you to before—meets Colm Fitzroy, he is dead set on taking over her family business. She's dead set on stopping him. Irresistible force meets immovable object. Colm is threatened now, having been betrayed in the past, and Pacer is just the man to save her while using the sweet, hot fire of his undying love to persuade her to surrender her heart to him. Pure dynamite!

Enjoy all our LOVESWEPTs—new and old—next month! And please remember that we love to hear from you.
Sincerely,

Carolyn Nichols

Carolyn Nichols
Editor
LOVESWEPT
Bantam Books
666 Fifth Avenue
New York, NY 10103

NEW!
Handsome Book Covers Specially Designed To Fit Loveswept Books

Our new French Calf Vinyl book covers come in a set of three great colors—royal blue, scarlet red and kachina green.

Each 7" × 9½" book cover has two deep vertical pockets, a handy sewn-in bookmark, and is soil and scratch resistant.

To order your set, use the form below.